The Lonely Cloud

The Lonely Cloud

RAJAN L. NARAYAN

PARTRIDGE
A Penguin Random House Company

ISBN: Hardcover   978-1-4828-4604-1
            Softcover   978-1-4828-4603-4
            eBook   978-1-4828-4602-7

Print information available on the last page.

To order additional copies of this book, contact
Partridge India
000 800 10062 62
orders.india@partridgepublishing.com

www.partridgepublishing.com/india

Contents

For Geeta.
If not for her,
I would have been one.

"High above in the deep blue sky,
In wonderful patterns of shadow and light,
Like cotton balls spun from a golden loom,
The winter's warmth scattered in the sun's light
A beautiful sight, to hold the eye,
How lucky they are, a collective sigh!
But far from them, alone he floats.
What troubles him, where does he go?
His beating heart some mystery holds,
He may return, in a different role.
Wherever he goes, may he never be lost,
That peace may find this lonely cloud."
(Rajan L. Narayan)

Acknowledgements

I would want to acknowledge the following
for making this possible.
My editor Mary Joseph for her crisp and brilliant work.
Sanjay Balasubramaniam for the germ of an idea and
for a lot of the detailing. Sudeep, Anil, Jayprassad, Raj
and Sachin for helping me with the cover. Renuka and
Udbhav for pushing me to improve my story. My dearest
parents for their unstinting support. A special thanks
to all my family and friends for their encouragement,
feedback and suggestions that have proved to be
invaluable.

Chapter 1

Sanju was so intent on the kite that he barely noticed her. The battle in the sky was at its exciting best and Sanju was moving with the silent, focused concentration of a 13-year-old boy in the middle of a kite-fight. It was touch and go, and so intent was he on the drama above that he just didn't hear her question. Even when it grew louder and more insistent.

There was a crisp chill breeze blowing across the vast playground. It was bang in the middle of winter and Sanju had a sweater on. The afternoons are the best time in winter to step out and warm oneself. Mornings are usually chilly and even inside the house the chill persists, almost right through the winter. In the afternoon people flock out of their houses to sit in the sun and enjoy a cup of tea. Sometimes neighbouring ladies gather to bask in the sun's glow and catch up on some gossip. But many afternoons are rendered dull by heavy smog that filters the sun's rays into a weak, listless and dull light. Such days are the coldest as the damp chill gathers strength and casts a deadly spell during the night, often claiming the lives of unfortunates forced to sleep out in the open without the protective warmth of even a plain simple fire.

But that day the sun was brilliant and golden in the sky, looking much like the handsome, indulgent father that he is. His warmth was calibrated finely, to counter the cold forest breeze that would otherwise chill a person to the bones. Now the breeze felt perfect. A gentle shiver ran through Sanju as the wind whizzed past him whispering 'hurrrrr' in his ears. Sanju caught the fragrance of the wintery forest air in it. He wet his lips and rolled his tongue over them to taste the sweetness of the forest. The trees at the fringe of the ground were swaying. Their leaves were rustling happily, sounding almost lyrical. The leaves looked and felt like emeralds in a perfect shade of green. They glinted in the yellow sunlight. Their energy was infectious and the birds were airborne, flying high in the sky, much higher than the kites that seemed to punch colourful holes in the blue blanket of the sky. Almost as though in play, the birds would swoop down to dodge between their papery guests, as if they were teasing the kites, daring them to come to life and compete with the birds. "What a life it would be to be a bird!" thought Sanju to himself. "How lucky they are, sunning themselves, flying and rollicking about."

Sanju could see his shadow on the hard red earth beneath. His hair was blowing in the wind; the sweat at the nape of his neck tickled his skin as it ran down the length of it. For a moment he considered removing his sweater but realised that he may misplace it and then he would have a lot of explaining to do to his mother who would lecture him about the need to be responsible and take care of his possessions.

The sky! Oh how beautifully azure it was! Perfectly, deliciously blue, like the inviting waters of a swimming pool. A perfect setting for yellow, red and green kites to buzz about pecking at each other. "Sarrrrrrrr," they moved about cutting through the heavy wind. The string in Sanju's hands was taut. His kite was tearing away from him. It was difficult for him to manage the pulsating *firkee* and the *manjha* so he dropped the *firkee* and let the *manjha* go. The kite took off and dived into the inverted pool above, the wind actually pushing the *manjha* which Sanju saw had bent into an elliptical shape. The manjha was racing out of the *firkee* now at a real fast clip, so fast that it cut Sanju's forefinger making him wince at the sharp pain.

In the sky he had gained the upper hand, more by luck; the other kite had swerved to dodge an opponent and his kite was now atop it! A thrill ran through him and he forgot the cut on his finger. All he had to do now was let the *manjha* run free and the friction and the weight of his kite would cut the opponent's *manjha*. He did that, but instead of the steady sound of a running *firkee*, he felt the sudden jerk and tension as the *manjha* stopped.

He turned quickly, his attention still on the conflict above, to see a girl about 11, completely tangled in the *manjha* from his *firkee*, looking questioningly at him.

She was speaking to him in Hindi, speaking so fast that he couldn't make head or tail of what she was saying. He felt his heart sink as his moment of triumph was reduced to ashes. He heard victorious yells from his rivals at the other end of the park and within seconds felt the string in his hand go limp as the boys began singing "Kai po che..." the song of triumph that's heard every time a boy takes down an opponent's kite anywhere in India.

Distraught, and silently cursing the girl under his breath, he began untangling the *manjha*, hoping the girl would go away. But she was insistent. He could make out that she was asking what had happened to his kite and if he'd lost it for good. He didn't want to talk about it and moreover didn't want to talk to her. He turned away, rapidly assimilating the *manjha* into the *firkee*. But she jumped into his field of vision, entangled as she was in his thread. He saw her clearly for the first time. She was plump and cute with an innocent round face in which were embedded large coal-black eyes. She was smiling and laughing. Her rounded hands holding bits of the *manjha* were held out towards him. She was wearing a frock with spaghetti straps, her hair styled in a close blunt cut that perfectly framed her cherubic face. She had cheap colourful beads around her neck, wrists and ankles. All of this combined to present her as just what she was: A pretty and vivacious child who one day would turn into a beautiful girl.

Sanju reached out and broke the *manjha* at various points to free the knots. He gathered it from her person, freeing her in the process, and regretfully threw the now useless *manjha* in a corner as he began walking away. Much to his surprise he realised she was keeping pace alongside him. He quickened his pace and she, mistaking it for a game, tried to keep up with him. He began running, only to be pursued by her, giggling and laughing at this exciting new game. Soon he was running hard, dodging past the boys and walkers at the park. He could hear her call out to him as she desperately tried to match his speed, he felt a surge of triumph at the realisation that he'd finally gotten rid of her.

Then he heard her cry out.

Instinctively he knew she'd fallen. "Good riddance," he thought to himself as he continued running. But he didn't get far. Reluctantly he turned and made his way back to her. She was sobbing softly, having tripped and fallen; she'd bruised her elbows and knees and scraped her chin. He knelt down next to her and gently began wiping the dirt from her wounds.

As he cleaned her wounds and dusted the mud off her clothes, a sense of regret washed over him as he realised he had held her responsible for no fault of hers. He recalled her saying something; perhaps she had been trying to tell him she was entangled in his *manjha*. But as he ran back and forth with the *firkee* in his excitement he had probably bound her even more tightly in the *manjha*. The more he thought about it, the more ashamed he felt of his actions.

"I'm sorry. I shouldn't have run like that. But I didn't understand what you were saying," he said in English. At once her sobbing stopped. She looked at him in amazement as she heard him speak in English.

"My Hindi's not very good," he continued. "We are from Andhra…" All of this brought no reaction from her; she continued to stare at him with a look of wonder on her face. Even the teardrops appeared transfixed in her eyes. All ready to roll but suspended in place by the same sense of disbelief that had gripped her.

He stood up, reached out and pulled her up and they began walking slowly back to where they'd first met. He didn't realise till much later that she hadn't let go of his hand even after they reached the spot where the girl's maid was frantically hunting for her.

But he did know that once he'd begun speaking, she'd gone silent. She walked the rest of the distance with her head bowed, strangely subdued except for a constant sniffing, eerily silent for someone who just minutes earlier had so much to say. The maid, like most maids, made sympathetic noises at her wounds and mildly castigated her for running away without a care. She warned her against doing it in future or suffering greater consequences than a bruised knee.

The girl barely appeared to hear the maid. Her eyes were fixed on Sanju. Feeling a bit out of place he asked, "What's your name?"

"Prerna," she replied with a shy smile. "Will you fly kites tomorrow too?" She asked in halting English. It was only then that it struck him that she'd been silent because she was working out the words, translating from Hindi to ask him the question in English.

Chapter 2

The steel frame of India. An apt description of the bureaucracy that runs this vast and seemingly unmanageable country. Along with the steel frame were steely tendons, cartilage, muscles and ligaments in the form of associated government employees of the hundreds of public sector undertakings that supported the steel heart as it beat deep in the body of the country.

Sanju's father worked in a public sector bank that symbolised the values and beliefs of the middle class in this country. Stern, nondescript and tending to silence, his father was typical of every father of that period. Why were fathers like that? Sanju often wondered. It was only much later that he fully understood how difficult society made it for men to strike out and be something different, and then he realised why it must have made sense for his father to be the way he was.

In a country where a bank job was a coveted one, it was perhaps better not to speak too much. There were too many jealous ears connected to nudging elbows and whispering lips. A word spoken carelessly could spark speculation about the integrity of the individual, giving grist to rumour mills. The community would be merciless in spreading the story, which would quickly become stories and with each passing be embellished with spicier details. Soon the information would reach the seniors at the work place who would need to demonstrate their decisiveness by taking action against the hapless and innocent individual. First he would be shifted to an administrative section of the office and then this would be followed by transfers to god-forsaken places or dead departments or worse a court of enquiry.

The politics of office, the fear of being implicated in a crime not committed, the pain of having to accept and comply with orders from a corrupt or incapable superior, coupled with the pressure of supporting a family and the expectations of an extended family perhaps ground out all conversation from Sanju's father. So there he was – a shadow of a man. Silent, stern and always angry, flitting away early every morning and returning home in the late evening to disappear into his room with his newspapers and magazines, emerging only for dinner, which was consumed in silent menace.

He did not believe in taking his family out, be it to the movies or dinner or on vacation, nor did he believe in celebrating anything. He believed that he was playing his role well, that of providing for his family. Beyond that he felt there was little he could do for them. The only time he displayed emotion was at the time of school results, when he would get animated and display his command over the English language to recall the duties of children towards their parents. His reaction would range from indifference – if the result was good – to rage whenever their performance slipped. As the children grew older and began asserting themselves, often disagreeing with him, he seemed to withdraw more and more into himself. Then he began using their poor mother as his conduit, lecturing her for hours on how he'd never talked back to his father as a boy and how such behaviour was a sign of future trouble. He'd often end these monologues saying he desired nothing from his children, only wanting to be left in peace without having his name and reputation sullied by the damaging and shameful actions of his good-for-nothing children.

Sanju was frank enough to admit that he had stopped caring about these lectures after a while. His father had grown so distant, spread so much negativity and sucked out so much energy that Sanju felt his family didn't have much holding it together. There was his mother who was always trying to keep the family in place by placating their father and getting the children what they needed. But this took a toll on her as in addition to this, she had to maintain her religious practices, which left her with no time to have meaningful conversations or to bond emotionally with her children.

That left Sanju and his sister; she was younger than him and was with their mother most of the time. Sanju's mother felt the need to protect her constantly. So she always hovered around the girl. Sleeping with her, going out with her, taking her to school and her various classes, leaving Sanju alone to fend for himself. So that was how Sanju grew up in one of those many nondescript small towns of North India. Alone, silent and often by himself. From school to college, college to university, university to a job – that would have been his life had it not been for the girl who got tangled in his kite strings one bright winter afternoon and changed his world completely.

Prerna slowly grew into his life despite no real effort on his part. As a native of Andhra, Sanju did not mix easily with the Hindi-speaking local boys. Many of the non-local boys in school were children of government officials and often transferred away. This left Sanju with a small group of boys he interacted with in his study circle whom he could call friends but not of the kind where any serious bonding happened.

Then came college. One attended college only during exams, or regularly if one was an active member of college politics which he was not. So Sanju was at home most of the time during his college years. And that's when he began to notice Prerna as more than the child he remembered her as.

She was a classmate of Sanju's sister, Deepa, and the two soon became close friends. Prerna visited a lot and on most days Sanju could hear them giggling and laughing around the house. Most of the time Sanju treated her with snooty disdain.

On Raksha Bandhan, Deepa came to his room to tie a rakhee as per tradition. Sanju noticed the presence of someone else; it was her very curious and shy friend. He could see her eyes flit around the room shyly, taking in the neatness and the order and also the posters of rock stars that stared out from the fraying paint.

She seemed really excited as Deepa tied the rakhee and collected money in return. She looked sweet in her traditional salwar suit. Something about her innocence made Sanju feel mischievous and he turned to ask her, "Why won't you tie me a rakhee?"

A stricken look flooded her eyes as she gasped, turned and ran out of the room. Sanju's sister sounded really annoyed. "Sanju, don't you have any sense? Can't you see how she feels about you?" she said and turned away to find and console her friend. He didn't think much of this incident and forgot all about it with the passage of time.

Then one evening, having just woken up from his afternoon sleep and realising he'd be late for evening classes, he rushed out of the room and raced down the small flight of stairs to the door outside which his bike was parked. Prerna at that moment was walking up those very stairs, humming to herself. Sanju ran straight into her and the momentum carried both of them down the stairs painfully as they rolled and bumped into each other and finally lay sprawled on the bottom step.

"Ouch, ooh mama....!" Sanju saw her wince in pain holding her hand.

He grabbed her hand and checked it for a break. It seemed fine. "I'm so sorry!" he said as he looked into her large limpid eyes now brimming with tears. Once again the tears seemed strangely suspended as they sat transfixed looking into each other's eyes. It suddenly struck Sanju that she'd grown into a beautiful woman. Her round face was flushed and pink, her lips were rich and quivering and her body felt warm and so soft. He felt his breath leave him and a sudden vacuum take hold of his chest.

Her fragrance, soft and delicate, wafted to his nostrils and he felt his world begin to spin around him. It was the moment of a lifetime. Time seemed to stand still. Oceans seemed to surge and crash in his ears. The light seemed bright and dark alternately. He felt as though he should simply pull her to him and feel her melt, literally melt, in his arms. She looked up and into his eyes. Her pain had apparently disappeared. In its place was a warm glow. A strange radiance seemed to emanate from her. Her lips curved to stifle a shy smile as her being felt the birth of his love for her. Her womanly instinct realised the significance of the moment. Her deepest wish had come true. The person she loved with all the sincerity that a woman could hold in her heart now reciprocated that sentiment.

11

"Ahem!" came a voice from the top of the stairs. It was Deepa. "I heard someone falling down the stairs, but I now realise that it was the sound of people falling in love!"

"Don't be silly, Deeps!" Sanju snapped, and then he turned to Prerna and said, "Sorry once again.... I should have looked more closely." The significance of the words he had just uttered struck both of them simultaneously and they smiled shyly at each other. Sanju turned and ran out to his bike. Something had changed permanently in him.

He was a man. He was a man in love.

Falling in love is not difficult. Admitting to it is. In India, especially in its smaller towns, love is acceptable in every situation except in the ones for which it exists. One can love cricket. One can love one's family. A man can, theoretically, love college, country, neighbour, grandmother – everything and everyone except a woman. That continues to be unacceptable.

Love, romantic love between a man and a woman, is strictly for poets to write about and Bollywood directors to depict on the local cinema screen. Families and young people rush to see the films and gush over them, sometimes weep over them. But once the movie ends, life is back to normal. That is a state that refuses to acknowledge the possibility of an emotion called romantic love.

A boy can talk to two kinds of women: the first is his mother or her equivalent – aunts, grandmothers. The second is his sister or her equivalent – cousins, 'rakhee' sisters. Talking to any other girl has to be strictly need-based. So if he needs notes from a classmate he asks her politely, "May I borrow your book?" and the matter ends there. If he is speaking to a friend's sister or a neighbour, he has to maintain a safe distance, never look her in the eye and direct his questions and answers at nowhere in particular. If an extraordinary request is to be made, it needs to be routed through the family. If a problem in class needs explanation from a studious classmate, his mother calls her mother or his father her father to make the request, and the answer follows the same route in reverse.

If a girl and a boy need to travel somewhere together, at least one parent accompanies them, usually the girl's mother. The boy's role is that of a guide, clearing the way and taking care of any menial tasks that need to be done. Once the need-based conversation is over, the boy and girl ignore each other.

Small town India has evolved a perfect system to tackle the problem at its very roots. The most effective way of preventing love is to ensure boy and girl never get to meet, of course. Therefore small town India often has a higher proportion of boys-only and girls-only schools and colleges. For coeducational institutions, girls go in groups and are strictly monitored by the families. Even for driving schools, girls-only ones are preferred or, in the worst case, the girl is accompanied by a family member.

This kind of conditioning and non-verbal cues has proven to be very effective. Girls rarely interact with boys, often avoiding them completely out of an unnamed fear of being called 'loose'. Boys on the other hand classify girls into two categories – the untouchables, who are the good girls, and a tiny set of girls called 'open' category. Any girl seen alone anywhere with a guy is almost certain of being stuck with this moniker. If the girl is seen laughing in the boy's company, it's damnation and if the girl is seen with any other boy or is seen with the same boy again, she is simply termed a 'pros'.

These are the unwritten but cast-in-stone rules governing behaviour in small town India. Go against it and one unwittingly alienates one's entire family from the community.

"Oh, that girl? Well... she had it coming you know..."

"Those parents were so fond of portraying themselves as 'modern' so now they have to pay the price."

"That boy's a wastrel, where is he likely to end up if he's busy taking girls to the movie halls? I'm sure that culture is in his family. Best not to have anything to do with them."

"Oh I've seen that girl, sitting out at night surrounded by boys, giggling at their dirty jokes. Why didn't she join a girl's college? Why does she need to hang out with boys? What do you expect to achieve sitting out with them so late! Can't she learn something good like cooking instead?"

"That boy! Keep away! HE SMOKES!"

Where love is denied light, water and care, how can it possibly germinate? Leave alone take root and flourish? Love between a man and a woman is actually considered bad. Even husband and wife rarely mention love. Duty is paramount. Love is disallowed. Married couples who display affection are frowned upon as being vulgar. A man can beat his wife and society forgives him. But it'll never forgive the man who kisses his wife in public. By denying themselves any expression of love for each other, parents set the most chilling example to children to avoid the 'L' word.

This castration of love is today called Indian culture and value. And Sanju – quiet regular sincere Sanju – had unwittingly walked into this alien world and was in the throes of discovering what it felt like and meant to be 'in love'. The enormity of his trespass hit him, after the initial flush of emotion waned. When, restless and uneasy, he slipped out and contemplated the future. It struck him that there was in fact no future. The dream was impossible, the word was banned and his emotions were sin. He tried to do the 'sensible' thing. Fought it. Denied it. Refused to acknowledge it. Refused to notice her, see her, talk to her. He avoided her. He felt weak, but told himself that this was best. This was what all boys did. Killed their emotions till they became bitter men-of-duty like their fathers, who refused to acknowledge the presence of emotion and preferred a world of motor automation.

But how could he avoid her when she practically lived in his house from morning to evening? He noticed her eyes, full of hope and affection; then as he continued to avoid her, their expression changed to puzzlement, and finally rested at longing.

This was more than he could bear. He decided to change tactics. What ignoring won't do, perhaps cruelty would. So he began acting mean, like a wastrel, a no-gooder, knowing full well that women shrank from such men. Put it down to his poor acting skill or his own lack of conviction, but he realised he had failed when one day, his attempt at smoking in her presence resulted in a fit of coughing. He expected her to laugh at him, instead she rushed to his side in concern and offered him a glass of water.

As he miserably gulped the soothing water, he caught the expression in her eyes. It was one of uncompromising love. Simple, pure, unfettered by the shadows that weighed on his heart. He put the glass aside and for the first time did something few young men had done in the heartlands, picked up her hand in his and raised it to his cheeks.

Before he knew it, she was in his arms and he heard himself say those forbidden words of the eternally doomed, "I... love you."

Chapter 3

For Prerna, there was no complexity in life. There was the one moment at the playground so many years ago that had decided her heart for her. After that her life was only about listening to the whispers that sang out from her beating heart. She hadn't thought it important to think beyond it. Few young women ever did and Prerna was no exception. It was most fortunate for her that Deepa was in her class in school and then in college. Their friendship hadn't been planned. They just liked each other and their common interests and tastes bound them into thick friends.

It's as though I connect with everyone in that family, Prerna thought to herself, happily. She was also liked by Sanju's mother, who found this lissom and hauntingly beautiful young girl very accommodating, helpful and well-mannered. Sanju's father behaved as though she didn't exist. The poor fellow was not sure how he was expected to react to his daughter's best friend. And the best way, he felt, would be to avoid the person in the first place. But over time even his ascetic demeanour wilted in front of her innocent charm. He would occasionally smile at her and give her some absolutely ridiculous piece of advice. Like the time he recommended she use castor oil for her hair. This wonderful insight was the result of overhearing Prerna and Deepa discuss the need to apply egg yolk to their hair. Prerna confessed her desire to do so but wistfully mentioned the improbability of its occurrence given her strictly vegetarian household where even eggs were considered taboo.

The memory of that incident often made Prerna giggle. She could recall clearly the lazy summer evening when she and Deepa rocked on the swing atop the Rao's terrace, trying to cool themselves as they talked of home remedies to battle the summer rash. Rao Saar (as he was popularly known throughout the town) was also on the terrace, seemingly involved in cutting bits of rubber from an old scooter tyre for some penurious application. He was in his customary summer dress, which comprised of a white vest that clutched at his narrow wiry frame and a white dhoti tied high on his narrow waist and folded up above his knees, displaying skinny white legs. His spectacles were on his forehead as he employed his old rusty scissors with great concentration to cut through the tenacious rubber tyre. He appeared so lost in his activity that the girls forgot his presence till he suddenly turned around in triumph.

In one hand he held the trusty scissors and in the other a rubber bit, "Eggs! The matter is not the egg or its yolk! The point is protein! Your hair needs protein. Look for a good source of protein! Yogurt, or almonds… or a good oil! In fact, the best oil for hair should be castor oil! No, my girl, don't worry about eating it, just rub it into your scalp and wash it off. That should be better than 10 eggs, I say!"

He then ran out with a smug flourish leaving a moment of silence before both girls collapsed in peals of laughter.

"Deepa, your father!"

"Prerna, your father-in-law....!"

Prerna looked at her best friend, her body racked with laughter, unable to speak; she gesticulated, "Where did that come from?"

Deepa, in the throes of her own laughter, managed to indicate, "From the bottom of your heart!"

And the lovely innocent young girls rolled in mirth on the hot terrace floor, enjoying their moment of camaraderie as the sky melted in love, high above them.

Prerna hadn't planned it at all. Her friendship with Deepa she felt was a happy coincidence, an indication by the greater powers that exist, that she belonged to Sanju and vice versa. And without much thought she merely went with the flow, happy to run over to Deepa's place daily to continue conversations from wherever they had broken off at school. She treasured those moments on the phone or at Deepa's house when she got a moment to speak to Sanju. She wondered why she always went silent when he spoke to her. Till a point was reached when he'd know that it was her calling even without her having to speak.

Sanju: Hello?

Prerna: (silence)

Sanju: (putting the phone down): Deeps, it's for you!

Prerna was never in doubt, only puzzled about why Sanju was taking so much time to resolve this for himself. She noticed his sudden silence, his withdrawal, his ridiculous new attire and weird behaviour and even wondered if he was trying to impress her not knowing how she felt about him. The reality was that she found Sanju refreshingly different from the other boys she knew – her brothers, her cousins, boys in the colony. Sanju was slightly shy and always so polite to her. He was never mean, never laughed at her. There was a kindness in him that she instantly warmed to. She felt safe with him. She felt he'd always be nice to her, protect her and take care of her.

And there was something else that she couldn't quite put her finger on, something inexplicable that drew her to him. It was as though she had always known him, always belonged to him. She always knew if he was at home or not, when he was somewhere close by, when he was looking at her and even when he was thinking of her. Especially that.

Sometimes at night when she tossed and turned in her bed, she felt she was there in his thoughts.

As though he was not lying on his bed,

But was on his bike, somewhere away from town but visible.

As though he was there on the peak of the hill,

Overlooking her town, and her room.

As though he was lying there beneath the starry sky,

Willing them to carry to her his messages of love.

As though he was longing for her,

Longing to tell her a lot many things.

As though he was listening,

To his heart and hers.

As though he was realising now,

What she had known years ago.

On a cold winter playground.

Chapter 4

Love was a culture shock for Sanju. He never realised that there was so much to talk about in this world. He wondered how so many things could all be so important at the same time to someone. Was there really so much to think and talk about when it came to choosing between blue bangles with a diamond design and blue bangles with a circular design? Who in God's name would be looking at a bangle's design when it was on the hand of someone as beautiful as her?

But he enjoyed buying bangles for her. He enjoyed buying cheap earrings for her. He enjoyed buying her an ice-cream and watching her eat it. He simply enjoyed watching her happiness. He enjoyed watching the deep flush rise from her neck and colour her cheeks. He enjoyed the meaningful flash of passion in her eyes.

He realised that contrary to what he'd thought, she was happiest with the tiny things he did for her. She seemed to have immense faith in his ability to take care of her. At times he felt uneasy at that thought. He hoped he could live up to her expectations, and provide her with her own home.

These thoughts coursed through his head as he sat with his back to the huge banyan tree on the sprawling college campus where she studied. It was hot and dry in the afternoon but the thick cover of trees provided sufficient shade even as the heat kept the population indoors. It was far from ideal but best for the two of them. They could meet and talk as long as they wanted. At least she could. He watched her as she talked. She'd been talking continuously since they met an hour back. Flitting from one topic to the other: some function at home, or some event at college or a cousin's visit. There were, it appeared, so many earth-shattering things she had to share with him that he never realised how the hours passed.

He didn't mind her talking at all. In fact, he was quite comfortable and used to it by now. He loved the excitement and the lilt in her voice. He found her laugh very attractive and strangely therapeutic. But most of all he loved to watch her. He was mesmerised by the roll of her eyes, the blush that rose from her throat and went right up to her eyes, the heave of her blouse, the nervous play of her hands, the feel of her head on his chest...

To him talking was a distraction, given their limited time together, so he would restrict himself to monosyllables or nods and shakes of his head. He didn't want to disrupt the feast before his eyes.

She knew it of course. The hunger and passion in his gaze as it devoured her, took her in completely, unblinking. A single message in his eyes. And the tension that built up sent a bolt like a powerful current through her when he touched her. And when he did that, she would go silent.

And he would take her in his arms and there she would melt as their passion consumed them, uncaring of the heat, the stillness or the incessant sounds of the mynas that hovered in the branches high above them.

They would meet on the campus or in parks like the one where they met the very first time. They had to be careful, very careful, because this was a small town where everybody knew everybody else and everybody wanted to be the first to report a budding romance and to have the perverse and frustrated pleasure of killing it.

Even though Prerna was a regular at Sanju's house, there wasn't much time they could spend together. Sanju's mother had a sixth sense for trouble and didn't want an affair right under her roof. So the girls were always under her watchful eyes and there was little Sanju could do except play the part of a disinterested brother.

But love flourished. For a few hours under the evening sky. In the sleepy alleys of the town library, sometimes with the permission of an understanding sister or in the noisy environs of an empty theatre. They met, made promises and violent love.

Sanju finished college and planned to write competitive exams for admission to MBA colleges. He knew he should be planning for a future, their future, but he was just not in a frame of mind to think or to plan. His life revolved around meeting her to meeting her again.

When he was not meeting her, he was thinking of her. He'd drive his bike to a hilltop on the outskirts of town and lie on the seat of his bike just watching the sky change colour. The blue would give way to orange and amber, stars would begin to show against the shadows cast by migratory birds. The grey would deepen, the air would get cooler.

Slowly a million pinpoints would come alive in the canvas above.

Sometimes the flushed sky would remind him of her face, the blackness of her hair, the shining stars of her smile, the coolness of her touch, the warmth of her breath. He would let his thoughts of her consume him, letting them flow into him, through him and out of him. Then he would make his way back in the darkness, exhausted but aflame.

Because both of them were so quiet otherwise, had so few friends and were so rarely seen or heard, nobody in that nosy town picked up the scent of their raging affair. Nobody walked out to the campus lawns in the searing heat. No one suspected that the girl leaving the house was supposed to have left it an hour earlier; nobody wondered where the boy disappeared to every morning.

And so their young hearts beat together and burnt together. With hope and dreams of realising their own little world. But they had been seen and marked – by the stars above, the unforgiving stars that rarely took the side of young lovers.

Even as they made plans and exchanged love notes, their doom was being chalked out in the cruel abode of the heavenly bodies, etching for them pain and separation. They hadn't yet realised that falling in love and living that love were very different things; it was a lesson they would learn. And how bitter a lesson it would be!

Chapter 5

Prerna returned from college with her final year exam time-table. The exams were a month away and she'd have to apply herself to her books to clear her papers. This had been a ritual for the past three years and she knew that clearing the exams would not be difficult. She was thrilled at the thought of finishing college but hadn't thought about what she wanted to do after that. She blushed. Of course, she knew! All she wanted was to collect her bags and move a few streets into the Raos' home. It was Sanju's problem after that, she thought to herself. He'd have to handle everybody.

With these happy thoughts she arrived at her house, only to be immediately accosted by her mother. "Where have you been all day, silly girl? Can't you stay at home one day? Now go up to your room quickly and put on your new dress... yes, the one you bought for your birthday. Don't worry, we'll buy you another... your father said so! We're already late for the temple!"

Prerna wasn't the kind to argue senselessly about such matters. She had an innate sweetness in her that made her

24

comply in most matters, not turning them into ego tussles. That did not mean she didn't have her own opinion. When it mattered, Prerna was very clear about how to handle an issue and usually had her way with surprising firmness. But accompanying her mother to the temple was hardly a contentious issue. In fact, Prerna enjoyed going out with her mother. They'd sit in the auto and chat about different relatives and the happenings in the town. Prerna's easy laughter would ring out and the driver would smile to himself at the sweetness of the moment.

So without much ado, Prerna flew upstairs and put on her new clothes. She took a few minutes to match the accessories as her impatient mother stomped below. All her mother's anger vanished as Prerna dashed down the stairs. She looked radiantly beautiful. The excitement of wearing new clothes and the run upstairs had bought a flush and glow to her face. Her eyes sparkled mischievously as she teased and ran around her mother with peals of laughter. Hearing them, Prerna's father walked out from his study and smiled to himself at his daughter's exuberance.

"She's so beautiful," he thought to himself. "And she's no longer a girl. She's grown into a woman... Where does all this lead to?" he wondered.

Prerna carried her happy mood through the trip to the temple. She was still giggling as they gathered the 'pooja thali' and climbed the stairs into the temple. There her mother's glare compelled her to stifle her giggles and she dashed aside to feed a laddoo to the temple cow ruminating sagaciously in its earmarked corner.

As she turned around she caught sight of her mother speaking animatedly to a youngish woman in her early 30s, who seemed very well off from her appearance. From the way she watched Prerna approach, it seemed the lady had come to the temple specifically to see her. Her attention was focused on Prerna and she wasn't holding a pooja thali or garland to offer the deity.

"Who is this woman?" Prerna wondered. She felt an unknown sense of dread creep up as her mother reached out and literally pulled Prerna to the woman.

"My daughter!" her mother couldn't contain her smile and looked unnaturally excited. The woman looked at Prerna and the full impact of Prerna's beauty hit her.

"How lovely you look!" she said as she instinctively reached out to caress Prerna's face. Prerna blushed in shy gracefulness, acknowledging what she believed was the kindness of a stranger. But the lady's next words shook her to the core.

"My brother too is very handsome! He works in the US and is here with me for the next two days. I was looking out for a pretty princess just like you for my prince and I'm so happy!"

She caught the look of disbelief on Prerna's face and said, "Arrey, looks like no one has mentioned this matter to our innocent little doll here! Look at her blush! Hi, I'm Sangeeta."

She then turned to Prerna's mother and said with complete authority, "Auntyji, I love your daughter and I think she is perfect for my brother. And knowing him, he will say yes!"

She continued, "We don't really believe in matching horoscopes. When my aunt told me about her neighbour's daughter Prerna who was beautiful, sweet and helpful, I decided to see her for myself. Now that I've seen Prerna, I'm fine to get them married right here and now!" She laughed aloud. Prerna's mother laughed in relief along with her but managed to add, "You know it is important for the boy and girl to see each other once and to get Prerna's father's consent. I've told him but he is the girl's father...," Sangeeta said softly, "Of course, we have to follow the customs. We will drop in tomorrow evening for tea." Prerna's mother was only too happy to comply and they left in a whirl.

Prerna suddenly felt weak. Did it really happen this way? She thought to herself.

The way it happens in the movies. Girl kept in the dark by her family till the boy drops in, the iconic tea that is served, followed by the heart-to-heart chat in which the girl is supposed to smile and look shy...

She wondered if she should tell her mother that very instant that she was in love with Sanju and intended to marry him. She wondered if she should sweetly tell the boy who was awaiting his afternoon tea not to expect more than a bitter aftertaste. She wondered if she should plead with her father for some more time before he banished her from her childhood home. A sense of the worthlessness of it all sank into her. She realised wearily how little she really meant to her family. They didn't see her as a being with emotions and thoughts of her own. Nobody in the house cared for what she wanted or bothered to ask if she wished for anything. Being born a girl in India meant being born to a pre-planned life over which a girl had no control. She wasn't seen as a contributor, merely as somebody who tied a 'rakhee' once a year, whose education wasn't important, whose views weren't considered on most things. Prerna felt hopeless. Utterly defenceless. Why was this happening to her? She could very well play out in her mind the reactions to her confessions.

Her mother would immediately inform her father and brothers and together they would take her apart. First emotionally, then physically. Her father would immediately contact Sanju's dad and inform him of their supposed folly. Her brothers would threaten Sanju. They may have him waylaid and beaten up to drive home the point of their masculinity. If he persisted, worse may happen to him.

And what of her?

She would be cursed, berated. She would be forever damned for this indiscretion. Abused, vilified, called all sorts of names, her opinion wouldn't matter. On the other hand, the resolve to get her married would only be strengthened. Her parents would blackmail her emotionally with threats of suicide. Her brothers would remind her that Sanju wouldn't be spared. She would be pressured till she just gave up or died. And to her husband this wouldn't be told. He'd rape her on the first night, give her a few children to look after in life and continue with his as though she didn't exist.

Her life would then be one of adjusting to him and his family. She realised that it made no sense to talk to her parents or brothers. They wouldn't give her a solution. They'd only increase her problems. This was something she and Sanju would need to handle.

Prerna decided to keep her cool and give no indication of anything, resolving to quickly bring this to Sanju's notice. He had promised to take care of her. Now it was his duty to make good his promise.

Time passed quickly and it was the next evening. She was handed a tray containing sweetmeats and asked to go to the living room. As soon as she entered the room, she could hear all conversations grind to a halt. Everyone, she realized was watching her.

She looked up and recognized her neighbour and with him was a family. An elderly couple, Sangeeta and a young man. Her neighbour nudged her towards them. The boy's mother smiled and asked her what college was she studying in. "Lohia College final year Economics" she said quietly.

"My son works at Magnysys at San Jose" she pointed at the young man

"After marriage, you can do your masters there," she said with a gentle laugh. Prerna stood rooted to the spot. She heard the boy gently chide his mother, "Relax Ma, give us some time..."

His voice galvanised her into action. She turned and fled the room. She dropped everything into the kitchen sink and without losing a single step ran out of the house.

She ran and ran till she reached the Rao's residence and even then she didn't stop till she'd run up the flight to Sanju's room and finally collapsed into his arms.

Sanju had no idea what to do. He was unemployed, living with his parents, a good 5 years away from considering marriage. He also knew what would happen if he went up to Prerna's parents to speak for their marriage. He would be immediately removed from the premises. With force if necessary. Prerna would be shunted away to a relative in some distant city where she would be married off immediately. All of this would happen at lightning speed.

And there was his own father to deal with, Sanju thought wryly to himself. He imagined breaking the news to his father and tried to think of what would follow.

"No wonder your academic performance never improved. How would it when you have other things to focus your attention on?"

"I must say I have been proved wrong. I thought you were absolutely worthless. But apparently you have some rotten skills. That of fooling young and gullible girls."

"Well what do you want me to do? Go about town proclaiming how shameless and useless my son is?"

"Like how you've found a girl for yourself, do me a favour and find a boy for your sister can you? Because nobody from our community would want to have your sister for their daughter-in-law"

He lifted Prerna's sobbing face from his chest, "Don't cry..." But she wouldn't stop; she kept sobbing and spoke through her tears. "I don't care what you do, I don't care what you want me to do, but I'll do anything. I only know one thing that I want to be with you only with you. I don't care about anything else. I would rather not live. Do something Sanju!"

Her hands gripped his shirt and as she shook it in her frenzy, the buttons, frayed and old, gave way under the intensity of its onslaught, flying off to bounce off the floor.

"We can't remain here" he heard himself say quietly

She stopped sobbing and looked up at him in surprise.

"It's pointless trying to talk to these people. They won't have any sympathy for us. They won't care for our feelings. They'll only do what they think is right. They'll send you away somewhere and quickly get you married off and my father will send me to a different town under some pretext and keep me there." She looked up at him at a loss for words. Her eyes questioning him for the first time since they'd met.

"We'll have to leave this place. This town and these people. Quietly we need to go away to some place where they'll never find us."

Chapter 6

They decided to elope the day after her last exam. That would give them time to prepare themselves and also make the most of her distracted family.

They also decided that Prerna would be non-committal about the alliance at home. She would use her exams as a ruse to sound distracted and pre-occupied and in that manner postpone the matter till after her exams. And once the exams were done with, they would waste no time in fleeing town.

Having said what he had, rather bravely, Sanju was coming to grips with the magnanimity of his words. "Let's run away." Was so filmi. It seemed so clichéd. Something said and over said in countless Hindi movies of the 80's, so much so that even Bollywood, that world of clichés and abused love-stories had abandoned the plot and the hackneyed phrase a decade ago. It felt very strange to be living a failed plot, thought Sanju to himself.

The heroes of modern Hindi movies were mostly successful men living abroad, driving fancy cars. Such men rarely needed to fight for their love as their women were independent, self-driven and didn't need parental approval to hitch up with these men. Moreover most fathers-in-law would only be too willing to hand over their daughters to such accomplished men. In fact modern heroes were now portrayed as having the upper-hand in such matters with the girl's parents reduced to playing their side-kicks and providing comic relief to the audience.

The other kind of heroes who ruled the silver screen played fearless police officers who sneered at love, an emotion that held no importance in a life dedicated to weeding out innumerable baddies from the country.

It was therefore left now to miserable, middle-class directionless boys of the country to play pole-bearers to the phrase. However all Sanju could glean from recent newspaper reports was that these compatriots of his weren't making much of a success of it. Society, it appeared had created many checks and balances to ensure such love-stories were nipped quickly in their buds often snipping off the life of the wanna-be hero. If the Romeo was lucky, he would get away with a broken bone or two. The other depressing aspect of the statistic was that the success rates dipped with the size of the town.

In cities, it appeared, there was more room for a romance to progress to successful marriage. Sanju's many relatives who lived in the metros were testimony to this truth. His family would occasionally receive an invitation card for a wedding taking place in a distant metro and he would hear his father's sarcastic tone underscore the name of the alien bride or groom and announce to no one in particular, "Ah, xyz is getting married. Another inter-caste marriage! I wonder if by the next generation, there will be anyone from our family of purely our community."

Then he would turn and look at his children sternly, "Don't you two dare to take this as acquiescence for your love marriage. Don't you two dare believe I'll sit by and watch you destroy our values. Not only will I not attend your unholy alliance, I'll never see you for the rest of my life!"

Sanju doubted if his father would come to his rescue in the event of his getting caught in flight. Something warned him that his father might even provide his assailants with the proper accessory to ensure a suitable beating. That was a depressing thought and Sanju felt restless with visions of himself lying unattended and uncared for in some derelict government hospital. Sanju's mind also dwelt on the possibility of the beating life may have in store for him at the hands of Prerna's family. Sanju had never really been in a serious fight besides a minor scuffle or two in school. He was just not the type to fight. Not a very mischievous boy, he had been well trained by his mother who repeated proverbs all day advising him to keep away from bad boys and situations that may create conflict. Sanju, being an obedient boy and lacking an aggressive instinct, had adhered to his mother's words and kept away from any situation that could lead to a physical altercation. Also Sanju himself disliked hurting people. He was a good football player and played for his college, yet never resorted to deliberate physical confrontation. He loved the game and always focused on the ball.

This was why he was well liked by most of his classmates. He had a non-intrusive, quiet nature that rarely challenged the norm. Sanju would slip in and out of college barely noticed. During college election time he preferred to stay low-key and not be aligned to any group. When approached by rival groups for his vote, he'd only nod his head and agree to vote for them. His athletic frame, calm nature and good looks weren't unnoticed by the girls in his class. But Sanju always had the acerbic words and unforgiving shadow of his father accompanying him and preventing him from making a play for any of the more-than-willing girls who regularly smiled at him, warm invitations for a coffee alight in their eyes.

All Sanju did was merely smile at them, refrain from getting into lengthy conversations and quickly flee the place citing some pending work; turning the warmth in their eyes into wistful yearning. Rather than putting them off, his diffidence, his shy smile and his display of good manners only made him a greater hit with the girls who'd break into immediate giggles on hearing his name and openly admit to their crushes on him.

There were the few who actively pursued Sanju. The phone calls to his house would increase suddenly. His group would suddenly leave him alone with a girl in the canteen, there would be requests for notes or a lift and a onetime love note on Valentine's Day: Sanju's reaction to all of this was regretful weariness. Like all young men his instinct was to grab what was on offer, but then his Freudian ego and the Hamlet-ian spectre of his father's moral ghost would harangue him continuously about the consequence till he made himself scarce to the girl-in-question and the situation.

But Prerna was the last straw. Even his iron defence proved weak before her unswerving love. He was unable to contain himself or his feeling or emotions for her. Like raging floodwaters breaching a dam, he was swept into her, in mind, emotion and spirit. He felt powerless in front of her liquid eyes, brimming with love for him and he could do little but quietly accept his role as little more than a leaf in stormy waters haplessly driven by a force far more powerful than he could ever grasp. The chain of events had led to a predictable play of events and finally Sanju saw himself doing exactly what he feared and had fought, most of his life.

While the plan to flee the town was made, Sanju had no clue about *where* to flee to. Most of his life he had spent confined in this town. They had been out on vacation just thrice in all these years. Once it was a wedding that had taken them to Chennai. The next trip had been a religious one in which his mother had visited Rameshwaram and a few other temple towns in the Deep South.

The third was the trip that they had made to Vizac, when Sanju was seventeen. That was when Sanju's grandmother had expired. She'd been living with Sanju's uncle in Vizac. Sanju's father was not on the best of terms with his brother and apparently not much closer to his mother either because Sanju rarely remembered visiting her and his father would rarely mention her or write to her or call her. Even the trip they made when she expired was bereft of emotions. They reached the uncle's house in silence. Took up temporary residence in a quiet room and just flung themselves into the funeral rituals.

There was barely any talk or conversations between the families. Sanju's parents were busy conducting the rituals over the 13 prescribed days. With guests streaming in, functions and rituals taking up large parts of the day, Sanju had really had no time to pay attention to the town or explore it.

Yet for lack of choice, it would have to be Vizac they ran way to.

Where would they stay there? Where would they find the money to set up a home? Who would get them married?

Sanju had no answers. It was now a destination point beyond which neither of them wished to think any more. Prerna was happy and excited that they had a plan. Nervous, yes, but hopeful of the outcome. Women have that ability to be content about the short term. In a way they were right because there is no such thing as the long term. Simply because life had so many probabilities that the long term seemed fantasy more often than not. Women lived in the security of the present and men worried about the insecurity of the future and often this was the difference between the two.

And so while Prerna left that night happy and content, insecurity gnawed at Sanju like never before. For the first time in his life he had to consider that big black strange world that was called THE FUTURE.

The future meant responsibilities. The future meant family. The future meant a decision. The future meant struggles, choices, options, a plan, a direction, obstacles, survival, failure, loss....

The future was here now. And Sanju realized with a sinking feeling that he was not ready for it. Desperately he fought the fears and doubts that his mind kept throwing at him.

Being caught at the railway station as they were boarding the train to Vizac.

Arrested for kidnapping a girl.

Where would they go to in Vizac? Not to his uncle's house surely?

He could imagine the shock on his uncle's face, the immediate call to his parents, the angry lectures, and the reprisals that would follow....

And how would he feed her? Where would they stay? He was penniless. Did that mean he would have to steal from his parents?

He felt physically sick at the thought of stealing from his mother. Because he knew there wasn't much money in the house, it would have to be her or Deepa's jewellery.

Once in Vizac how would they get married? Where would he find a job? Surely the money he'd stolen won't last for more than a week. Then what?

What if he was arrested for theft? He knew his father well enough to consider the probability that his father may want him to spend some time in prison for this act. He'd heard of such horror stories about prison that the thought made his stomach churn. And what of her when he was behind bars? A doomed life, shunned by both her family and his? Who would care for her? Would she be turned into the streets? Or forced to marry someone? Would she take a drastic step then? His mind recoiled at these thoughts that continued to bombard him day and night.

Finally the evening arrived. Their plan was to take the midnight train. That way both families would be fast asleep. And they would have a clear eight hours, by which time their train would have crossed into another state. They would meet at the station a little before the train came in and board it separately so as to not raise any suspicions. And yet he had resolved nothing in his mind. He was racked by insecurities and worries. For himself, for her and for them. Then he thought of his parents and his father especially with all the scorn and anger on his face shouting aloud when he hears about the sordid affair,

"That useless wastrel! I knew he would end up doing something like this!"

This picture was so sharp in his mind that it shook him and he lost his resolve and the courage to go through with the plan. His mind threw him the lifeline

What if you don't go there tonight?

Prerna would reach the station, not see him there and return home.

What would happen then? She would blame him, hate him and break up with him....

It was a painful thought but to his worried and terrified mind, it was a problem of a much smaller impact.

The end of their relationship.

It would hurt him terribly but he deserved it, he thought.

As for Prerna, she was better off without him. A few years later, at San Jose she'd probably forget all about him. This was reality. How it really happened in life, he consoled himself as he felt exhaustion and sleep overtake his tired mind....

An incessant banging woke him up. It was morning and someone was banging on his door!

He opened it, his mind still numb from sleep and saw the stricken face of Deepa on the other side.

"You didn't go?!!" She almost shouted at him.

Dumbly he shook his head as the enormity of his actions sank in.

"You knew....?" he stuttered

"Of course, I knew everything... Prerna is my best friend...

Where is she?"

"I don't know..." before he could complete the sentence he saw the shock and anger on her face. "But she hasn't returned since last night. Her family is all over town searching for her... she was spotted at the station...."

For the first time he saw an expression close to disgust on his sister's face. "You were never worthy of her... if anything happens to her...," and she burst into tears and fled down the stairs. Sanju saw her collide with his father who had returned from his walk. He was stunned to see his daughter crying so hard. "What happened ma... tell me," he spoke gently as he hugged her.

Together they left the staircase and entered the living room where Sanju heard his sister tell his father everything through her tears.

He had nothing to do or to say. Zombie-like he went to his bed and sat down on it. His head held in his hands. His mind was reeling, flashing images at him.

The first day in the park when he met Prerna

The day he collided with her and noticed her for the first time

Their moments in the lawns, park and in different hidden parts of the town

Her smile.

Her laugh.

The gentle heave of her breast.

The softness of her feel.

Her tears as they streaked down her face.

Prerna.

His inspiration. Lost forever.

He heard his father climb up the staircase and open his door. He looked up and for the first time in his life looked into his father eyes. There was no anger on his father's face.

No menace, no rage.

No questions or doubts

The expression on his face was simply conveyed by what issued from his lips.

Two single words that summed up the truth.

"You coward."

Chapter 7

Sanju came awake instantly. It wasn't more than five hours ago that he'd crept into his bunker, exhausted and bone-weary. But now he was instantly alert. It was still dark outside, the ship moved stealthily as it was meant to. In a few minutes it would be abuzz with activity. Sanju was always the first up in all his years at sea. Silently and briskly he prepared for the early morning drill. At the break of dawn, the entire ship was deep in the course of drill. A half hour respite for breakfast and then they reassembled for the morning chores. The combination of work and drill never lost its pace right through the day, with only a short break for lunch it continued till the sun set.

This was their final month at sea and all the fresh rations were exhausted. The entire crew was living off canned food. The only time they had to themselves was the few hours before bedtime. But Sanju was always the first to volunteer for service even at this time. There was always something to be done on the ship and Sanju never stepped away from the most back-breaking or the most dangerous jobs.

Exhaustion and work were drugs to which he was now addicted. The constant pressure to stay alert drove away every other thought that entered his mind. And that was what he yearned for because, try as he would, he could never forget. The memories were fresh as the morning dew in his mind and no amount of control could drive them away. After five years of trying he knew the pattern and was wise enough to accept that there was no point fighting it. The only way to overcome the torture of those memories was to be under constant, immediate pressure and danger.

The human mind is designed for self-preservation and when threatened it has the ability to focus its every part on identifying the source of danger and devising methods to overcome it. Sanju welcomed the pain of being constantly on the edge, surrounded by danger.

He had made it to the naval academy three years back and had volunteered to join the MARCOS. Six months of intense training was something only he seemed to relish, as over 60 per cent of the volunteers dropped out, unable to take the gruelling ordeal.

A marine commando's training has no simulation. Every bit of it is real. Because no amount of simulation prepares an individual for actual action. And a critical situation is no place for a MARCOS to learn. There isn't any scope for error. A MARCOS cannot afford to say, "I didn't know that this would happen," or "I hadn't planned for this situation."

So everything the MARCOS team did was real. This called for a certain kind of profile. A MARCOS is everything an army commando is with the special skills of handling quick operations on water. In short wherever water was involved, MARCOS would be in operation.

Given the extreme and gruelling conditions, volunteers from the officer cadre were typically in the 23-25-year age bracket having the right mix of experience and youth with a record of having led a unit. The volunteers from the rank and file were a few years younger but having joined the navy earlier had more experience on their side.

The training was rigorous. The Indian armed forces are rarely cushioned with the best gear. While the weapons were fit for the task, the accessories were kept at the basic level, often little more than canvas and hemp. This kept the unit as close to natural elements as possible. The MARCOS training involved living in the wild. Here they had to survive with absolutely no support and eat off the land. Very often there was no choice. Lizards, rats, weed, whatever was available. They were trained to distinguish what was poisonous and what could be eaten.

They had little or no comfort, were trained to eschew it, in fact. To be focused and objective-driven, they were to treat everything other than the job at hand as being of tertiary importance. The only thing that was a reality in their lives was the presence of pain. A raging, searing constant pain.

The pain of injury, of partly healed wounds; the pain of the dead weight of a brother commando slung across the shoulder; the pain of an adversary's sharp blade; the pain of muscle, brain, sinew, blood, bone.

The pain of fatigue. Of being powerless.

The pain of expectation

The pain of bearing a critical burden

The pain of responsibility

The pain of losing a brother commando,

The pain of failure

The pain of having failed the unit

Sanju welcomed the pain. Fresh as he was from his own personal hell, nothing was enough punishment. He pushed himself. Often he was the first to take up a task. His eyes dead, his body uncaring. When the pain hit, he would bite it back, drinking in his shame. His father's eyes would sear his mind, his sister's tears would burn his soul and he would find the strength, the self-loathing would fill him with the capacity to take in the pain and he would soldier on. There were many moments during the training when he almost died. When he'd been rescued in the nick of time. His commanding officer was often nonplussed and in fact often discussed Sanju with his superiors.

"What's niggling at you, Anand? You're worrying about that boy Rao, aren't you?" Rear Admiral Nair always cut to the point. And this evening at the academy was no different. He'd walked in to the dining hall and noticed Cmdr. Anand pacing outside the main hall.

Anand looked up; the old guy never missed anything. I wonder where he got his information from, he thought. I was just waiting to talk to him about this. Cmdr. Anand still recalled the final training session that Sanju's unit had performed. As their commanding officer, Anand had designed the entire programme. This was the ultimate test of power, endurance, skill and team work. No person can work on his own, a truth applicable in every walk of life. There are no stars, only successful teams.

Yet just as individuals in sports and in professions believe they are primarily responsible for all successes, likewise the military units suffer officers and individuals who believe they are the superstars who can win an entire war on their own capabilities. Often such people cause grief and are detrimental to their teams despite their superior skills. Intra-unit rifts lead to poorly executed plan and failure of critical missions. Anand knowingly created his final programme as a test of teamsmanship as much as of courage, resilience and skill.

The situation involved Anand himself being held hostage on a floating barge that was sailing towards a fall. The team was given 14 minutes to rescue him with enemy fire breaking out at regular two-second intervals and enemy commandos popping up across the riverfront. Failure meant their commanding officer would hurtle to his death or get killed in the crossfire. This was no simulation. This was for keeps. It demonstrated the absolute trust and faith the commanding officer had in his team. Every team inevitably underwent such a final test and emerged successful on every occasion. However, never before in the history of the MARCOS was a test designed that was as dangerous as this one.

Anand, sitting in the doomed barge, calmly recorded the entire pandemonium as it broke out around him.

He saw the mad dash, the crazy stunts, the incredible performances that the MARCOS team undertook to achieve the objective. It would be the first failure of a MARCOS mission. Had it not been for one man.

Sanju Rao.

Putting himself at the gravest risk, Sanju plunged into the water in a desperate last effort, destroyed the dummy terrorists on the barge in a trice and pulled Cmdr. Anand out just as the barge tipped over the 50-foot fall.

Anand remained unruffled as they were pulled ashore by the team. There was a long silence with only the roar of nature heard. The team, spread out as they were across the wilderness, knew nothing of what had finally happened. But all of them had heard the crashing of the barge as it splintered at the base of the waterfall. They all gathered in silence on the river bank close to where the rest of the unit were strewn in exhaustion. It was only much later that word got out of the incredible effort on the part of Sanju that had saved them from eternal damnation.

They celebrated the next day late into the night. But two people quickly made their exit from the raucous celebration. One was Sanju, who appeared to shrink at such events and quietly made his escape. The other was a more thoughtful Cmdr. Anand. His mind replayed the chain of events on the barge. And what he concluded after careful evaluation disturbed him. He needed a second opinion. He needed to sound out a mind better equipped and better experienced than him in such situations.

There was none better than Admiral Nair. He'd got his opportunity and cautiously he vented his worry. "That's right Sashi," Anand replied slowly, knowing that Nair preferred to be addressed by his first name at informal gatherings. "Something's not right about him."

"What's the Doc's opinion?" Nair asked

"Well that's the problem. He says the boy is fine, clears all his psych tests, but...."

"But?"

"I can sense a problem there. I work with him every day. And you know it's not just Sanju I'm worried for...." That last line got Nair perked up, "You want to explain that?"

Anand nodded and continued, "I wonder if Sanju's pent-up emotions will one day put his brother MARCOS at risk." He looked deep into Nair's eyes and the question lay there. Right there between them for years and years. Silent and unanswered.

Sanju graduated and was posted first in Kashmir, then in the Andamans, then in the Indian Ocean and wherever he went he seemed to follow the action. He plunged in fearlessly, almost with a death wish. But every time he emerged successful and victorious and often risked his life for his fellow MARCOS, pulling them out of hopeless situations. But he'd shun the congratulations and celebrations that would follow. He'd disappear into some corner of the world where no one could reach him.

Almost as though he was disappointed at having survived.

Chapter 8

The late evening sun was orange and huge as it sank into the placid Arabian Sea. Its rays seemed to wreak havoc with the climate of the city, making it hot and muggy like only Mumbai can be on May evenings.

Sanju had taken an instant liking to Mumbai. Not that it was a charming city. It was overcrowded, narrow and uncaring. The summer made it unliveable as sweat poured from people in streams and dust and diesel fumes clung to their skin like leeches, clamping down into their pores and then rotting as the bacteria thrived on the moist pulpy material, letting loose a range of smells that hung above the city like a devilish shroud, pervading tightly packed trains, buses, gyms, malls, cinema halls, sinking into seat covers and bedsheets, clothes and swimming pools till inhabitants recognised each other by that smell. The smell that hits a visitor as his train snakes down the Ghats and enters the city. That very smell that blasts into the pressurised cabins of aircraft as the hapless hostess opens the door to let passengers out.

Sanju was looking forward to the monsoon. Still a few weeks away, it was, he believed, the best time in the city. Especially the first rain. The first rain is kind to Mumbai; it washes away the grime that covers her and hides it in the puddles; Sunday afternoons are ideal to drive around in the rain. Gothic structures and green treetops stand out against a dark gloomy sky. "And then while driving around her empty streets, you just might catch a fleeting glimpse of the great beauty she once was," Sanju thought to himself. Mumbai was like a yesteryear Bollywood diva: a city of unrivalled charm and beauty; a city, once at par with the best in the world. But she hadn't been the soft and delicate type. She was at once ambitious and ruthless; lusting for power and money. And in her heyday she had it all:

the fawning crowds, the big, imported cars, the madly-in-love heroes, the choc-a-bloc diary, the adoring industry, the plethora of endorsements, the endless list of lovers, the infinite one of admirers.

Then one day it was all gone. The utter self-centricity that consumed her, that consumed her inhabitants, moved on. Suddenly she was passé, over, a commodity. A joke for spot-boys to snigger about. A ghost that inhabited a lonely forgotten apartment in a quiet, unknown bylane of a forgotten suburb. Watching her own old movies and lamenting at the inability of the world to recognise her yet-abundant talent. Mumbai, once so exquisite, then ravaged and traded raggedly by the merchants of mammon and now, in her late middle-age, left uncared for, dug up occasionally for some forgotten treasure and left untreated. Her wounds open festering sores yet unable to hide or obliterate her innate beauty.

He jogged as these thoughts crossed his mind while he alternated between marvelling at the city and cursing her. No other city could take your breath away and at the same time evoke a curse word. But life here was good for a naval officer. Navy Nagar was at the southernmost tip of the city, its prettiest part. Set amid green trees, quiet churches and calm seas, Navy Nagar was coveted as much for its serenity as it was for the infamous life that the city believed its inhabitants led.

It was a self-contained little township with quarters for officers and staff, messes, offices of the naval brass and the popular United Services Club where they all congregated for an evening drink. The Navy Ball that took place in the last week of December was once the event that people would kill for. But over time, it was completely forgotten, overshadowed by the more glamorous and glitzy happenings at the 5-star hotels in the neighbourhood.

Sanju was unconcerned with all this. When he wasn't at sea, he kept himself occupied with training to keep himself battle-ready. If not doing work, he'd be doing his drill, honing his skills and perfecting his tiny errors. And every evening he'd leave for those long runs. Whenever Sanju looked back at how the intervening years had changed him, he often wondered if he was the same laid-back, chilled-out Sanju from a small town with no plan of action in mind.

Was he?

He sighed, his reverie broken by the angry honking of a car that narrowly missed him.

Sanju was on his evening run, having left Navy Nagar when it was still afternoon, run right up to Worli and now returning through the gates of Navy Nagar. He was in a shaded woody part, about 15 minutes from completing his run when he saw a figure emerge from the trees about 40 yards ahead. Something about that figure was familiar.

It couldn't be.... But it was!

Mehul.

He couldn't hold back the loud whoop that emerged from his lips, his tired legs found a spurt of energy as he found himself running those last few yards.

He could see the smile broaden on Mehul's face as he began chuckling. Sanju launched himself on Mehul, jumped onto his friend as a little child would, his legs crossing over Mehul's torso. The momentum of his weight was too much for Mehul to hold and they both lost their balance and fell on the grass amidst their laughter.

"*Kaminey kab aaya?* When did you get here? Didn't tell me anything, yaar! Not fair."

Mehul was still smiling. When he smiled his face, which everyone called the ugliest in the world, turned into the most radiant piece of luminosity that ever spread light.

They were sitting on the grass. Sanju, his legs spread out and body supported on his hands propped behind his back on the ground, was breathing heavily, exhausted by his run. Sweat poured from every pore. His shorts and tee were completely soaked. Mehul was in slacks and shirt, chewing on a strand of grass, legs bent at the knee. Sanju looked at him and wondered if there was ever anyone he'd loved as much as he loved this guy.

His best friend, brother, advisor, guide, saviour....

Mehul was probably the most loved guy on the base or on the ship, or in school, in the mess... everywhere. It stemmed from somewhere deep inside him, Sanju thought as he studied his best friend, talking animatedly. Mehul was pure. In his heart and his soul. He instinctively knew what was right under any circumstances and knew what to do. And he did it without malice or ill will towards anyone.

And so for every act of bravery Sanju did out of despair, Mehul did more with compassion.

If Sanju accomplished incredible records, Mehul earned the deepest love from fellow sailors.

If Sanju was fearless, Mehul didn't let fear enter into the equation. If Sanju courted danger, Mehul rescued people from it. Sanju risked his life to prove a point, Mehul made a point of saving lives. Sanju pushed himself and the limits harder, Mehul drew people to himself.

They were the two most popular young men at the base. One admired and feared, the other loved and honoured. And each cherished and respected the other for being what he was not. As brother MARCOS they often conducted sorties together. Their teamwork was impeccable and their record outstanding. Because each knew the other would back him to the end, putting his own life on a limb if the need arose.

Which they often did but never talked about later. Yet the other always knew. Not about the specifics but just knew. It had been like this for years.

But something has changed today, thought Sanju to himself. There's something on Mehul's mind and he's going to tell me in a while. He's thinking about how to break it and what to say. He's wondering about my reaction to that and what his response should be.

Why do things get so hard? He wondered. And for Mehul? Who usually knew exactly what to do and how to conduct himself.

Mehul was an orphan. He was a casualty of a riot, one of the many that plagued the country. He had been rescued by the army platoon conducting flag marches in the riot-hit town. With no one claiming him, he had been taken back to the army base and cared for by the CO and his family. The CO moved on in a couple of years but the boy stayed and was adopted by the regiment. He studied at the school, lived in the barracks, did odd jobs and won everybody's affection. The regiment chipped in for his college after which almost automatically he chose the military and volunteered and trained with the MARCOS as he was an excellent swimmer.

Mehul could never hold anything back, so radiant was his essence, neither would he be in doubt for long, thought Sanju as he saw his good friend, ponder, lost in thought

Then almost as though in cue with Sanju's thoughts, he saw Mehul shake himself as he came to a conclusion. He watched the doubts fade from his friend's countenance as the radiance re-emerged on his face. Mehul turned to Sanju and smiled like the sun emerging from clouds.

"Sanju, I got married my friend. I wanted you to be the first to know."

Chapter 9

Sanju waited a while before the impact of the sentence hit home. Mehul was married.

Somehow he'd envisioned both of them as being confirmed bachelors for life.

What do you feel when you best friend gets married?

You don't feel. You know. That despite your buddy's best efforts to maintain the status quo, it won't remain so. For all his insistence that nothing changes, it does.

For all your attempts to do the same things all over again, the fun would've gone from it. The point is that there were two of you and what remains continues to be two. Only you aren't one of the two. And that's only appropriate, Sanju thought to himself. Friends don't lend respectability. A wife does. Society begins looking at a man with renewed respect. In fact with marriage is when a man's view is taken seriously. He's considered responsible. Sensible. Respectable.

Two young men house hunting in Mumbai would be hard pressed to find one to rent. Most society office-bearers cast them out unceremoniously. Most owners frown and shake their heads.

Wastrels.

Drunks.

Trouble.

But for a young married couple, doors open miraculously.

How cute!

You're just like our daughter!

The society is here to help you. Please remember to attend our Sarvajanik Ganapathy festival this year!

It takes time for this truth to sink into the mind of the freshly minted husband. Most Indian grooms sit up late on their wedding night drinking with their friends in an attempt to show how little would change in their lives.

But everything changes. Not like the sudden change of night into day, more like the gentle transition of autumn into winter. Slowly the man evolves, learning new things every day. Understanding the meaning of warmth and gentleness, of the need to consider the feelings and emotions of others.

Few things improve a man like the close association with his infinitely better half. Few things cause such a tectonic change in a man's behaviour and attitude as marriage does.

Things will never be the same, mused Sanju to himself. Then a thought struck him.

Mehul said he *was married* not engaged but *married*. Sanju wondered how this had happened. Sanju had a family, however distant, yet a physical bunch to take it upon themselves to get him married. But he was single. And here was his best pal, an orphan, who had somehow got married. He raised his brow enquiringly at his friend.

"Who on earth is your kin to have taken that much trouble to arrange it for you?"

Mehul's smile widened as he let loose the next shocker, "Arranged *kahan*? This is a pure Indian love story!"

Sanju was floored. Literally. His hands slipped from behind him and he fell back on the grass with a loud thud. "*Kya baat hai!* This is fantastic. *Ekdum chuppe rustom nikle yaar!* We've been together so many years, so many years you never told me a bloody thing! How many years have I been stupidly unaware of this?" Saying this, Sanju pounced on his friend and pushed him to the ground, pretending to strangle him. Mehul, laughed at his friend's astonishment, "*Bas yaar, baaaas bas*! I'll tell you, I'll tell you! We've been in love for two years now. It took some time for things to settle, fall in place between us, and to convince her folks.... You know how families are. Everything is about caste, community... and here I was, an orphan a sailor at that. It took time but finally they relented. And once that happened I wasted no time. Immediately got married!"

Then he spoke in a much softer tone, "Forgive me Sanju, I know I should have called you for the wedding but everything happened so fast. Yes, I'm guilty of not telling you about it in the course of the last two years. But I didn't find the right time maybe, or I felt things were not in a shape to be shared. Sometimes we don't like to talk about our private lives – future, present or... past."

When he said that last word it struck Sanju that Mehul meant something by 'past'. Sanju realised that Mehul was possibly hinting at his own silence about his past and his reasons for being what he was. Being so close to him, Mehul must have worked it out that what drove Sanju was something from his past. He was far too intelligent not to have noticed his penchant for taking on dangerous tasks. But being a sensitive human being and a caring friend, he had never once asked his friend about his past or the reasons behind his brooding silence. He had merely adapted to Sanju's whims and mercurial temperament and made a success of their friendship. But that was Mehul, warm, sensitive, brave. Sanju wondered about his wife, how would she be? Would she have a problem with their closeness?

But that would change, anyway. It always did after marriage. No more late night booze sessions, no more reckless adventures. Maybe fewer dangerous missions as a team?

"So where's bhabhi? Left her at her parent's place have you?" he teased his friend.

Mehul looked surprised, "No way, she's here! Why would I marry her if I were to leave her with her folks?"

Sanju jumped to his feet, "Chal, let's go right away. Today we'll have home-cooked food for the first time in our naval career!"

While they were walking back, Sanju kept shaking his head in wonderment, "Boss you're the real deal, two years of a love affair! But where did you meet her? When did you get the time? How did this all happen?"

"Arrey yaar, I met her many years back, we kept in touch casually, then as we got to know each other we realised we had a lot in common. We began to correspond and whenever I got time, I'd go and meet her. For a long time there was no commitment on either side, we were happy just to know and explore each other. Then one day I realised how much she meant to me. You remember that Kashmir incident? It was just after that. I realised that my life could have ended without my having told her how much she meant to me or knowing if she really loved me. So I took a few days off, met her and proposed to her. She was ready with her answer. And then it was simple, all I had to do was to win over her family. That took time but now I have a family of my own for the first time in my life."

Sanju looked at his friend, who seemed so happy. Usually a person who was happy for others, for once Mehul was genuinely happy for something that had turned out right in his own life.

Sanju was genuinely happy for his friend. I hope this works for him, he thought. I want every bit of joy that's possible to be in my friend's life. And I'll do anything for that to happen, he thought to himself. He wondered how his own life would have been without the stabilising and calming influence of Mehul and he wished him the best.

May everything I have be yours, he thought. May the joy of marital bliss that could never be mine be yours... before he could complete his thought, they crossed into the row house in which Mehul lived.

Even though it had been years, the woman standing at the entrance of Mehul's home was so familiar that Sanju didn't need a second glance to know who it was.

Prerna.

Chapter 10

Sanju's mind was in a whirl. He had no idea, no clue what to do. A million questions, a hundred million possibilities. No answers.

Almost as if it was the Day of Judgement, thought Sanju to himself.

Not a day passed when Sanju hadn't anticipated meeting Prerna or getting news about her. Sometimes even at the most critical part of a mission, almost as though to kill the unbearable tension, his mind would be dragged to thoughts of her. Sometimes visions of standing above her corpse would float into his mind, sometimes he would see her being raped and violated brutally, and at times it would be her silent questioning eyes. Once when his body was racked with pain and he slipped into delusion, he felt her presence next to his. But not his loving, caring Prerna. This was an avenging angel, uncaring of his pain and oblivious of his repentance. She didn't want answers from him. She only wished to watch him suffer. See him writhe in pain. The physical pain was exacerbated by the mental torture the sight of her put him through.

He was in enemy hands and they were putting him through the wringer, trying to extract information out of him. It was hell. No training can help you deal with pain. No theory, no psychologist, no method. There's nothing that can be repeated or discussed. There's only the mind that welcomes it. For Sanju the pain was catharsis. It was the punishment for his sin. For his cowardice. For his weakness. For his crime against Prerna.

He had loved her and ditched her. And he had received no punishment.

This was it. It should kill him. Then free him. But before it killed him, it had to inflict maximum pain. Unbelievable pain. Tearing pain. Unbearable pain.

Sanju opened his mouth to scream in agony but all he could hear was her name from his ravaged throat like the guttural shriek of an exorcised demon. He screamed and screamed and laughed in incredulity to find he was still alive. He welcomed the pain. His teeth were pulled out, his fingernails pulled out. His arms and legs broken.... But he was still alive.

If Mehul hadn't broken in and killed his tormentors, they'd have gouged out his eyes, smashed his testicles, pulled out his tongue and skinned him alive. But even that he would have withstood. For no one was as hard on him as he himself was and no one knew the extent of his self-loathing. And no one knew of the love he had for her.

Had he died that moment he'd have had her name on his lips. And for that he would have been happy. Had his enemies gutted him, he'd have accepted it as his deliverance. Sanju regretted that one thing about his life, that he encountered love first and then the ability to withstand pain. This sequential order had cost him his heart. For had it been the other way around, he would have had her.

But here was the strangest of paradoxes. The limit of his pain was yet to be tested, he realised. For his saviour was also his executioner.

It took enormous effort to remain silent and inexpressive. His training helped him here. The ability to quickly divert the mind from the throes of doubt and focus on the real helped him manage situations that threw the three of them together. Like the first day they met. And subsequent days when he was invited for dinner or when they dropped in at his house.

But it was a pressure situation. He knew he would not be able to sustain himself over a long period. Something would snap and his control would break. The problem was that for the next six months he was at the base. There was work but it was easy compared to the gruelling time-table of the battleship. It was also a break from pattern to be at base and not to be seen with Mehul. And it was difficult not to interact and meet Mehul and Prerna, especially because of the naval base's close familial environment.

There were parties, dinners, get-togethers organised by some officer and it was impolite not to attend, also Sanju and Mehul had been regulars at such events in the past as they welcomed the opportunity to dig into home-cooked food. So for Sanju to avoid such gatherings would raise questions. Moreover how many could he avoid? If he went for some and avoided others those friends would feel very offended. And given the camaraderie that prevailed at the base, it was something unthinkable. So Sanju found himself often running into Mehul and Prerna at social events organised by the members of the fraternity.

Sanju would greet his friend and Prerna cordially and then beat a hasty retreat to some corner of the party. For the hosts and guests, Mehul's marriage was the talk of the base, and most people were eager to greet them, meet Prerna, help them set up home. There was something enchanting about a new bride. There was always so much hope and brightness around her. Fortune and luck were considered to follow a bride to her husband's home.

The naval community was close and treated every member as family. And Mehul was very popular, he was liked, respected, loved. His seniors considered him a model officer, their wives looked at him as the son, brother or friend they could turn to for anything knowing he would honour their trust with every drop of blood in his sinewy body. Every teen and young boy wanted to be like him. Every girl took his help for school/college or work projects and every kid landed up at his house in their spare time to build ship and plane models with him.

Mehul loved them all genuinely. He considered them his own and therefore never seemed to miss a family. His doors were always open. Like his great generous heart and his battered, bruised, effervescent face. This large family welcomed Prerna with open arms and she seemed to be the perfect match for Mehul, seeming to add to his affections, and their popularity as a couple soared. They were wooed, pampered, made the cynosure of every gathering, loved, feted and cherished as the model pair in this close-knit community.

And Sanju slowly slipped into the corner. Beyond the attention span of everybody. Here he took respite with his thoughts for company. And now they returned with a ferocity he could offer no defence against. They raged in his mind

How did they meet?

Does Mehul know about our past?

How much has Prerna told him?

They have been in love for two years?

They? That includes Prerna? Does that mean she does not love me any more?

And why should she, he thought to himself bitterly, after what I did to her?

What happened that night?

Sanju thought back. Prerna remained missing for some days. Then one day the people of the town were shocked to hear that her father had sold the house and the family had moved away to some unknown destination. An entire family had been uprooted due to him. His cowardice.

And no news about Prerna. Dead. Or a situation worse than death?

He had been eaten up all these years by these thoughts. He still didn't know. He was none the wiser. Because he got nothing from Prerna or her eyes. They were calm when they looked at him. Giving nothing away. He only knew one truth. That despite all that had happened between them and all the years that had flown past, despite whatever she thought of him, he loved her. Still. And he wanted her for his own.

Chapter 11

Sanju hated the truth. But he knew he was a prisoner to it. He had failed Prerna once and now he was going to do it all over again. The last time he had failed her by not turning up and claiming her and this time he was going to steal her from her legal and lawfully wedded husband.

Had he really stooped so low? He asked himself.

To know himself for a coward was one truth he still hadn't come to terms with and before that was resolved he knew himself to be a thief.

Stealing his best friend's wife. That would be comparable to Vaali, the mythological king of Kishkinda, as described in the Ramayana. Vaali quarrelled with his younger brother, Sugreeva and threw him and his friends out of the country over a misunderstanding, yet retained Sugreeva's wife and kept her as his own. That single act of his cancelled out the many brave, daring and heroic deeds he had done till then and ultimately led to his assassination by Rama, the Prince of Ayodhya and the hero of the Ramayana.

In the legend, Rama kills Vaali whilst hidden from him as Vaali is fighting Sugreeva in a duel. Angry at being felled in such a dastardly manner, Vaali curses Rama for contravening the code of battle and calls him ignoble and unworthy of being king.

Rama's answer to Vaali was perhaps the clearest explanation of dharma and duty that Sanju could ever remember reading. Rama fends off Vali's accusation and reminds him that as king and older brother to Sugreeva, his duty under every circumstance was to give his brother a rightful hearing and most importantly consider Sugreeva's wife as his own daughter, treating her with love and honouring her, whatever be the activities of her husband.

In contravening this postulate, Vaali had committed a grave crime for which his punishment was death. The delivery of that death did not need to follow any code of conduct. It was punishment for an act of utter shame.

Sanju cringed at this thought. Right through his childhood he had always been fascinated by the character of Vaali. Vaali was everything Sanju was not. He was incredibly brave, utterly fearless, and very fierce. Vaali was impetuous and wore his temper on his sleeve. Vaali didn't wait to be challenged, he was the kind to seek out his enemies and finish them in their homes. Once a terrible demon called Dundhubhi challenged Vaali at his doorstep. Vaali at that moment was making love to his wife after having consumed a lot of wine. Uncaring of his own state of undress, Vaali rushed out on hearing Dundhubhi's call. The demon, observing Vaali's still erect member and noting his inebriated state, offered wryly to return the next morning so that Vaali could have one last night of pleasure with his wife. But Vaali only laughed devilishly at Dundhubhi's suggestion and rushed at him, delivering a most horrible death in the course of the next few minutes.

Alas, thought Sanju to himself, all my life I wanted to be as brave and courageous as Vaali had been. But unfortunately the only act in which I'm like him is the one that shamed him and caused his ruin. That of coveting his brother's wife!

With conflicting thoughts of lust and loyalty coursing through his mind, Sanju was in a terrible state. Knowing what was right, yet being powerless to do it, once again Sanju found himself spiralling towards taking the wrong decision. If earlier he had been weak and not stood up to his duty, here he found himself being weak and flowing with the erroneous tide, too gutless to even attempt swimming against the tide.

Thoughts of her consumed his mind. Run, man run, he told himself. If he ran hard earlier, he ran like the devil now. Tiring himself to exhaustion. He wanted to drive any thought about his friend's wife out of his head. It's not right, he told himself. She's someone else's wife and that someone else is the one person you love the most in your life, your friend, brother. The man who you've trusted blindly with your life and who in turn does the same. So forget her, get her out of your head. Think you never met her, you never knew her. This is someone else.

But Sanju was to learn the hard way that the brain and the heart sometimes operate at odds with each other.

The mind can tell us what the right thing to do is but our emotions make us do something else. And we do it knowing it is not right. We are compelled to do it. In full consciousness and in complete control of ourselves, we do wrong. And the more we do it, the less guilty we feel. We begin to justify our actions. And Sanju too found enough in his armoury to justify his continuing attraction to Prerna.

He knew her from before. He loved her from before. She loved him.

She loved HIM.

That was the truth. She loved him, Sanju. She always had. Mehul was a compromise.

When he looked at it like that, he suddenly realised that indeed it was he who was the wronged party.

He and Prerna were meant to be together. Not just now, always. And one incident should not be the reason for their separation. Their future was together. And her presence here was a sign, an indication of this greater reality, this cosmic truth that Prerna was his and belonged to him. And it took his best friend to find her and bring her to him. Sanju had no doubt now that he had to win her back, rekindle her love for him. Once this was done and they were committed to each other, then he would gently break the news to Mehul.

And he knew Mehul well. The moment Mehul heard about their past and their love that was built over decades, he would step back. And Prerna would be his.

How powerful is the mind! It can create an entire world of lies and deceit and falsehood so cunningly and methodically that this world becomes the truth. So it was with Sanju. He believed in this alternative reality, the more he believed in it, the more it appeared to him that his belief was true.

Prerna's every action and word was twisted in his addled mind to further this cause. A casual smile from her was construed as an acknowledgement of love. An invitation of dinner was an invitation to meet her. A casual greeting on the road was an attempt to rekindle the flame.

His mind was so consumed with her and he began believing in this lie so much that he believed it was just a matter of asking for her to accept and he tossed and turned to get an opportunity to meet her. He began sending her text messages to which he received no reply. He called her but got no response. He took these as her inability to reply because of Mehul's presence. He could bear it no longer he wouldn't wait any longer.

And one day he got the opportunity. It was at a party they were attending when suddenly Mehul had to leave to attend to a call. He requested Sanju to drop Prerna home.

It was a longish walk from the Mehra's to their block. At one quiet corner, Sanju caught hold of Prerna's hand, "God, it has been really long. I love you so much and know you do too..."

She broke away from him in controlled fury. "How dare you! Don't you know I'm married? To your best friend who you claim is a brother to you."

"But you love me, I know that. You are mine. You belong to me. Mehul will understand this."

Her voice took on a strange flat metallic tone when she replied. She spoke in a soft low voice, but it carried to him clearly in the night.

"I have no idea what you believe in your sick mind. But I want to make one thing clear. I am married to Mehul. And I will always be his while he is alive. You have been trying to reach me and I ignored your advances thinking you would get the hint. But clearly you haven't got the message. So let me spell it out clearly. Don't try and contact me in any capacity except as Mehul's wife. Don't you dare ever touch me or grab me in future. I don't intend to talk about today out of respect for your relationship with Mehul. But if you message me or try to touch me again, I'll tell Mehul and register a case of molestation against you. So keep your dirty hands and filthy mind off me."

Chapter 12

The briefing took place en route to Bombay High. Far into the sea, these rigs were India's sign of oil exploration ability on the high seas. Their puny output was not a drop compared to the needs of the nation. Yet it was a matter of pride and it was oil.

There were a bunch of rigs adjacent to each other and very often, workers had to move from one rig to another as a part of their work flow. Movement from one rig to another was done as per stipulations of a standard operation procedure that had stood the operations at Bombay High in good stead all these years.

This involved workers forming a queue at the point of embarkation. From here they would be led in single file along a well traced short path to the boat that was to carry them onward. Once all were safely in, the captain of the boat, a veteran of many years at sea, would follow a pre-charted path to the desired rig. The boat would approach the rig as per a preordained path and dock at the point of disembarking. Here again the workers were trained to disembark in an orderly fashion. All this went on day in and day out over many decades without any major incident or accident. But then there's always the law of probability that hovers over every action that finally decides to chuck one tiny ball at the end point of the bell curve. And on that dark stormy day everything that could go wrong didn't, except for one tiny spark. But that was enough.

The rigs drill out crude oil, and despite their best efforts to prevent leakage, there's always a visible or invisible film of extremely flammable oil around the rigs. That's why the rig is treated with 100 times the safety precautions of a petrol pump. Because a single rig was like a million petrol pumps together, sitting on tons and tons of oil.

Despite all the precautions, it happened.

What led to the spark?

Was it from a match thrown carelessly by a cold passenger desperate for a smoke?

Was it that as the boat approached the rig, its metal side rubbed against the metal structure of the rig?

Was it a bolt of lightning that struck the oil floating around the rigs?

The answer would never be known. On that unfortunate day, all it had taken was a tiny spark and the catching up of the law of averages and a raging fire gripped its main platform, on which were trapped men, material and the control system of the entire platform.

Although it was a fire fighting job, the violent sea and irregular topography made it impossible for the regular firemen and coast guard to mount the platform. And even if they had the spirit to attempt the rescue, they'd only end up killing themselves, thought Sanju wryly to himself. The fire fighting system in India had remained exactly where it was when the British left the country.

Fire fighters were called firemen and treated like watchmen, without respect. Their uniforms and gear hadn't kept up with changing times and technology. There was no yellow fireproof material covering them from top to toe like in most other countries. They still wore prehistoric Greek helmets made of the heaviest fire-friendly metal. And if their brains weren't cooked early enough, their cheap rubber boots would melt in a jiffy to ensure they remained rooted in pain to the spot till they were fried by the flames.

Firemen still sported thick canvas tunics, making movement incredibly tough and without any facial protection gear, their eyes and skin were singed instantly the moment they were brave or foolish enough to approach the unrelenting flames. Few of them received adequate training and very little of that training was for the kind of conditions they encountered during a real outbreak.

Their training manuals hadn't kept abreast with the changing topography of the city, hadn't adapted to the narrow lanes that constituted the suburbs, couldn't fathom the complexities of modern structures and had absolutely zero support at the local level. Most apartments and office structures flouted every possible fire safety norm. Building plans were rarely available, air draft spaces were quietly consumed and the internal area was often changed, modified and broken up in defiance of fire safety. All of this comes to the fore during a raging fire. The brave firemen reach late, delayed by traffic and narrow roads that prevent the fire engine reaching the apartment block-in-need, then dash in, try their best to save lives. But this leads to nothing. The problems are followed up in the newspapers for a few days then forgotten as life returns to its old flagrant ways.

For firemen, fighting fires on land was an uphill task and on the rigs they would truly be literally at sea. More a hindrance than help despite their bravery. The coast guard were only good to round up straying fishermen. That left protection and safety of the rigs squarely in the hands of the Indian Navy. Sailors doubling up as firemen.

Usually MARCOS were not needed for such operations as regular sailors and choppers were sufficient. Those trapped in the rigs were trained to wear lifejackets and jump into the seas. Choppers would drop tiny floats for them to hold as groups till a navy ship could come in and pull them aboard using ropes. However in this case some key personnel had been at the rigs and were trapped in the fire. This required the MARCOS to be pressed into the operation. They were needed to go deep into the rigs and seek and rescue these key personnel. Rescuers would be air-dropped into the rig, to search and locate the stranded, then strap them or lead them to the drop zones and then load them on the choppers flying above or direct them to the sea where the coast guard boats would pick them up.

Coast guard and naval choppers as well as boats were fully immersed in the operations and it was felt that the MARCOS team would be needed to be dropped into the platform to complete the rescue operation. The boys were always ready for action especially to help their fellow countrymen. Moreover the people at Bombay High were always considered special because of the risk and rigour they underwent in such inhospitable climes.

Four of them were in the chopper that whizzed to the rigs 160 km from the Mumbai coast.

Only Sanju was perturbed. In his mind, he kept playing out his last conversation with Prerna. He refused to believe that she meant what she said. It was her pent up anger at his rejection, he told himself. She loves me and is merely angry with me. It will cool off. I just need to give her some space and time. He looked up to see Mehul keenly observing him. He arched his brow questioningly, "What's been on your mind, yaar? *Tu kabse khoya khoya hai.* Snap out of it. We need to be really alert down there."

Sanju nodded. He wondered about Mehul. Somehow he felt Mehul's presence had just complicated it for all of them. Prerna's mind is stuck because of her marriage to Mehul. If Mehul wasn't in the picture she'd accede easily. She's after all a 'Bharatiya naari', he thought wryly, it must gall her to be thought of as the woman who ditched her hubby.

Sanju believed he needed to keep working on her. If only Mehul wasn't there! His life would be so much simpler and all that he ever wanted in life would be his!

"Approaching station Alpha." The voice sounded over the din. The four of them with practised ease approached the chopper exit. The chopper hovered over the flames at a spot near the steel girdles. They'd need to shinny down the rope to the narrow platform on the girdle and from there use the girdle frame to reach the cabin below.

Eight people were trapped in the cabins. The oil pipes needed to be turned off. Some safety installations cleared. Some important documents and records collected. They'd split their teams. The other two MARCOS would shut the oil flow and close all mechanical levers and collect the documents.

Sanju and Mehul would lead the personnel rescue.

Together Sanju and Mehul reached the cabin. They broke in and located five people. They roused them, treated them and took them to the chopper point. Here they strapped them to the ropes and sent them up the chopper.

The chopper's capacity was four people and now with an additional person, it flew away. It would be hours before it returned. Which meant the remaining three would need to be pushed into the sea. After a protracted search, Sanju and Mehul located two of them. Mehul's task was to lead them to the platform from where they needed to jump into the sea. Sanju's was to locate the last person.

Sanju was deep in the bowels of the rig. Although the other MARCOS had done their job, the fire was out of control and most of the rig was in flames. The situation in the cabin was impossible. Sanju located the last man, who was unconscious. Strapping him over his shoulder Sanju was trying to find his way out when the cabin collapsed in flames. Sanju fell unconscious.

He felt someone rousing him. It was Mehul! Mehul had returned to fetch him. He pulled himself up and, carrying the man, they slowly made their way out. Mehul pointed to the girdle through his mask. Sanju understood they had to take that up and hope the chopper returned soon.

It took them hours to make it to the top above the flame. If it hadn't been for Mehul's indefatigable energy, Sanju felt he'd have died. They waited at the top, holding onto the girdles. Sanju was on one and Mehul on the other a few metres away. They held on hopelessly. Suddenly over the noise and the smoke they heard the sound of the chopper! In minutes they'd be safe!

The survivor was coming round. Sanju was holding him strapped to his back. Suddenly Sanju heard a loud sound above. He looked up to see one of the girder plates had come away and was swinging towards them with tremendous force.

It was a steel girder and weighed about twenty tons. It would reach them in seconds. Sanju knew from his training he needed to reach out jump at it and deflect it. It would surely break but that way he'd save Mehul.

Every commando does it to save his brother. If Sanju swerved it would reach Mehul and if he too ducked it would swing back and sure take Sanju on the rebound.

6 months ago Sanju would have leapt at it without a thought. But now, for that fraction of a second a face came into his mind. He didn't leap but swayed away. As he did he turned round and knew what he would see.

Mehul had unflinchingly leapt and was on the girdle that tethered dangerously then shuddered as it broke at its pivot. His eyes met Mehul's. Just a few feet from his.

They were calm and unwavering. Sanju heard his voice float over the din very clearly.

"Sanju. Marry her."

And then the girdle broke and, together with the bravest man the navy ever had, was swallowed in the unquenchable, relentless flames that had risen from the innards of hell.

Chapter 13

Everything had changed. Or perhaps nothing had. Sanju wondered why it hadn't been he who had died on the girder. Why is it that the better man had to die?

He envied Mehul. In life Mehul was loved by one and all. He was admired, respected, looked up to and won the love of his wife. In death he achieved immortality. His act of bravery would soon be turned into a legend. His shining example would be quoted in all training material and codes of conduct. He would be honoured posthumously and awarded the Param Vir Chakra. He lived like a god, was loved like one and would be honoured like one for eternity.

But then all of this wasn't what Mehul ever wanted or cared for in his life. Sanju doubted if Mehul would even have been comfortable at the thought. Mehul always did and acted without ever wondering what people would think of him. Mehul did what he believed to be right. Mehul did it because he liked to help people. He believed it was his duty to stand up for those who couldn't help themselves. He was the perfect and archetypical naval officer.

Mehul had gone into the inferno unconcerned about himself or his young wife. He saw himself as duty-bound. Even as he returned for Sanju, he had quietly displayed his innate heroism and his act on the girdle indicated a soul that had transcended the realms of human affection, relationships and bondage. In his actions and in his parting, he had made life easier for Sanju but at the same time more difficult. Strange it is, thought Sanju to himself; living with Mehul for so many years didn't inspire me as much as his death had.

Had Mehul guessed? He wondered. Why did he say what he said? In his final moments as death approached him, had Mehul had a thought for Prerna and wished her to marry again? Did he instruct Sanju because Sanju was the only man there? Or was it because he knew? Or was it because he believed Sanju would honour his word and marry his widow, still an uncommon practice in India?

Whatever the reason, Mehul had in dying cleared the path for Sanju, it appeared. Not only was his absence a removal of the guilt and negativity in Sanju's approaching Prerna, but also his instruction to Sanju provided him with a stamp of authority in approaching and wooing Prerna.

All very good in theory or for a love-crazy me, Sanju dryly thought. He recalled his state of mind on the chopper and was suddenly filled with shame and remorse. He felt disgusted with himself. How could he have stooped so low? How could he ever have harboured those thoughts? I always find new depths to sink to, he felt.

Another part of him laughed in disbelief. Look at you! it screamed. When you had the opportunity to have Prerna you ditched her. When you should have avoided her, you chased her, now the route is clear and you're running away! You're pathetic!

What about Prerna? His last conversation with her came to his mind and a fresh sense of self-loathing crept into him. But there was something he had to tell her. At the right time.

For now, there was very little Sanju could do but stay away and let Prerna get over the tidings.

Mehul's body was never recovered. It would have been a miracle had it been, such was the blaze which consumed everything on the rig; therefore the rites were performed without it.

The entire base provided a protective cover around Prerna. Nobody wept or cried. That was a value of the Navy. Because Mehul had died bravely he was honoured, celebrated. He was cherished and would be remembered and missed. The light that he lit with his unbridled enthusiasm and infectious personality would be carried forth by the children of the base who had been touched and impressed by him. For the next few months, Sanju too was busy and was then assigned to battleship duties again. Six rigorous months later he was back. Almost a year had passed since that day on the rig. Right through this time, Sanju had been struggling with many conflicting thoughts.

But on top of everything were Mehul's final words. He knew exactly what Mehul meant. And that was the quandary in his head. That intertwined with the image of the girder hurtling at him and him ducking. He knew that the flow of events was being keenly studied and scrutinised by the war room. But more than anything he knew he had to meet Prerna.

She was not at the base. She had shifted out. It took a month of searching to finally locate her in Pune at Deccan. She was teaching now. At a school for orphans. She had found employment with an NGO there and lived close by.

One evening as she was wrapping up her correction work after most teachers had left she felt a shadow fall across her desk. She looked up and drew her breath. Standing at the entrance with a thoughtful expression on his face was Sanju.

"Hi Prerna." He spoke slowly, "It's been a real long time.... I searched a lot for you; I was recuperating at the hospital for a month or so."

"Yes, I know, second degree burns, they said," Prerna spoke in a measured tone.

"That's not a problem," he shrugged "I needed to see you, to meet you...."

"Why?" she said. "I never wanted to meet you. I made that clear in our last conversation. I have nothing for you. I don't want to interact with you. And now that Mehul is no more...."

Her voice cracked. But she controlled herself with an effort, "Now there's nobody to connect and link us. So why should you want to meet me? Since I don't want to meet you."

It was his turn to speak, "It was not like that Prerna. It is something that Mehul said to me before he died...."

She looked up at him stunned.

His voice was a whisper, "Mehul asked me to marry you."

She flinched as if he had hit her. "That is impossible! Impossible, you hear?" she spoke violently, "Because you don't know a thing!" She paused, as if speaking to herself. "It was my mistake. My mistake. I should have told you earlier. The last time we spoke."

"What?" he asked.

She turned to him with a controlled anger that flashed in her eyes, "That Mehul knew. He knew about you. About us. All the time."

"WHAT!!" he screamed.

"Yes. Do you know how and where we first met?" she asked cruelly, roughly, "It was exactly at the place and time I was to meet you to start our life together... so many years back."

"NO!" he screamed again.

"Yes," she continued. "Let me tell you what happened that fateful night when you left me at the mercy of the elements and the cruel world. Let me tell you the full extent of your cowardice. Let me see you cringe and know the full extent of the damage you did to me. And let me paint a picture of your friend Mehul and why he is and will always be what you are not and can never be."

Chapter 14

There was a chill in the night air as Prerna quietly slipped out of her home. There wasn't a soul out on the streets at that late hour of 11 pm, which was unsurprising because the town usually wore a deserted look by 8 pm through most of the year and an hour earlier in the winter. There were many months yet for the onset of winter but the heavy incessant rain had succeeded in bringing down the ambient temperature and Prerna shivered as she made her silent way through the alleys.

It was very unlikely she would get an auto or cycle rickshaw at that hour, and she would have hesitated to take one even if it was available, for this was a small town and there was always the possibility of being recognised by the auto driver. Young girls in small towns rarely travelled to railway stations in the dead of night unless accompanied by their family members and a suspicious auto driver may, purely out of concern, inform her parents. But the station was no more than 15 minutes from her home and she made it there on foot with about half an hour to spare. Having anticipated that she would be walking to the station and not wanting to be slowed down along the route, she was carrying nothing more than a single shoulder bag.

The station was empty, save for a couple of porters half-asleep beneath the ticket counter, long since shut, in anticipation of passengers alighting from the midnight train. The very train she was to take, hopefully to fulfil her one and only wish, since that day when she had found herself snared in Sanju's kite-strings. Prerna's eyes wandered along the length of the station. At some distance from the entrance of the station was the solitary food stall, ubiquitous to all railway stations across the world. This snack hut was partially open or partially closed depending on how one wished to look at such matters. A few people were loitering thereabouts; travellers waiting for their connecting train, not wanting to spend money on a hotel room for a few hours and some lost homeless souls who only found shelter in lonely, forgotten railway stations or under their connected bridges.

This town was proud of the fact that their railway station was accorded the distinction of being a 'railway junction'. This meant that it had five platforms in all; the main platform which opened onto the street, two more across from it and finally the last two, built recently, further away down the tracks. It was on one of these two that the midnight train was expected.

Prerna didn't know where to wait. She didn't have a ticket, therefore couldn't enter the waiting rooms so she decided to wait outside, but then it struck her that the sight of a single woman waiting alone on the main platform could draw the attention of a railway attendant. She enquired with the porters and was told that the midnight train would arrive at the distant platform. The sight of the dark and lonely platform made her heart sink and reluctantly she took the overbridge leading to it. As she reached the top of the overbridge, almost on cue the sky that had been threatening ominously all through the evening to unleash its fury opened up with torrents of rain in sudden rage, replete with sky-shattering lightning and thunder.

Caught unawares and without any rain protection, Prerna ran the rest of the distance in desperation but was soaked to her skin by the time she reached the largely uncovered platform. Miserable at her condition, on the verge of tears, she groped her way towards the bit of shelter pausing there to wipe herself with her totally inadequate little handkerchief. She now had nothing else to do except shiver as she waited imprisoned by the merciless rain in the darkness. As time passed by and the clock struck midnight, she grew more anxious looking around for Sanju in desperation. But the cruel night refused to heed her prayers and no Sanju arrived; no light broke through the inky blackness and no hero rode out to smite the looming evil. As the seconds agonisingly moved on, slowly the thought took root in her innocent mind that perhaps he might not turn up at all. The idea was so debilitating that all strength left her feet and she clung to the cold wet metal column for support, stifling the sob that rose to her lips.

But fate was not yet through with her for the night. For startling her from her sorrow, screaming down at her at a mind-numbing speed, tearing through the curtain of rain with an eardrum-shattering shriek that drowned out the howl of the angry rain was a one-eyed black demon of a train, spewing fire and sparks. To her terrified eyes the train was not just a hell-hound but pure hell itself on iron wheels, towering above her, dwarfing her very existence, disorienting her mind and draining away all energy from her with its primordial power.

The rain, the train and the pandemonium froze her mind and she shook and quivered, rooted to the spot. The train slowed and ground to a screeching halt and the door of the coach closest to her sprang open as some men jumped out from it. They looked rough and reeked of alcohol. The sight of Prerna, cowering and wet, seemed to ignite dark visions in their heads and after a quick word with each other they moved towards her with the intention of making a grab for her.

Self-preservation warned Prerna and she turned to flee. One of the three men moved very fast and grabbed her. She screamed but he cut her short by covering her mouth with his thick, hard hands. Like a twig, the three of them lifted her, kicking and thrashing, into the train which had begun moving by then. Soon they were inside, it was a 2nd a/c coach but since it was not vacation time most compartments were only partly occupied and the few occupants were fast asleep and unable to hear Prerna's struggles over the sounds of the train and the storm outside.

They dragged her into their compartment as she began kicking and screaming. But there were three of them and they handled her roughly, slapping her a few times to shut her up. Then they gagged her so that she almost choked and bound her tightly, leaving her like that on the floor of their compartment. They didn't dare attempt the rape inside the train for her screams could attract other passengers or the railway guard, instead they decided to get down at the next station, take her to a secluded spot and then disappear. They spent the next hour in excited anticipation, drinking heavily, and eagerly looking out of the window or rushing to the door at every approaching station to see if it was deserted enough for them. Shortly, as the train drew into a station, the men decided not to wait any longer and after furtively checking for movement within the train and at the station, they picked her up and rushed out of the train.

As the train began leaving the station, the coach door opened once again and a lithe, athletic figure jackknifed through it. He rolled on the platform and sprang up again in one fluid motion and began to give chase to the three figures that were making slow progress on the overbridge with the struggling girl. Their struggles with the girl as they exited the train had woken him up and when he saw them holding the struggling girl on the platform, he took the call to pursue them in an instant. He watched them bundle her into a taxi and speed off. Now his mind was made and he was certain that this was a kidnap or something worse. Rather than search for a policeman, he decided to take matters into his own hands. He jumped into another taxi and barked an order to the sleepy driver to give them chase. The crack in his voice was warning enough for the driver to know that this man couldn't be denied. So he obediently set off in pursuit.

The chase lasted almost two hours. The taxi carrying the kidnappers slowed down when they were miles into a lonely hilly road. Dawn was on the horizon when it drew to a standstill at a bend on the road. Two of the men got off, and approached the pursuing taxi which had halted a few yards behind it. The third man held a struggling Prerna in the car, as he watched his companions approach their pursuer who had gotten off and was walking towards them in smooth and quick moves.

"Stay out of this, bachchey," growled one of the kidnappers, "There won't be enough pieces left of you to fit in a towel if you don't run away," he flashed a knife with practised ease at the approaching man.

Before either of the men could say another word the young man, in a single move, was upon them. His leg came down with tremendous force on the knee of the knife wielder who dropped to the earth, clutching his knee in mortal agony. In the next second the man's fist had struck the companion three firm blows on his jaw, solar-plexus and groin putting him out of action for months.

He jumped to the taxi ahead, flung open the door of the taxi, pulled out both the driver and the third man simultaneously. The driver cried out his innocence and retreated to a corner. Three swift kicks rendered the third man immobile. The man looked into the taxi at the terrified girl and spoke softly and calmly.

"Don't worry. You are safe. My name is Mehul. I'm a commando in the Indian Navy."

Chapter 15

They drove back to the town the kidnappers had alighted at. There he took her to a restaurant that was just opening. It was still early morning. He gave her fresh hot tea to drink and water to wash her face with. She was shivering and had a blank expression on her face. When he returned after paying the shopkeeper he saw she was lying stretched out and still.

When she came to, she was in a hospital. It was a clean room, fresh breeze blew in from the window and sun streamed in. She looked across to see Mehul asleep on a chair at the foot of her bed, his feet resting on the end of the bed. The events of the previous night flashed through her head. Did all of that actually take place a few hours back?

Memories hit her like physical blows.

The coldness of the night, the lonely walk to the station, the bitter chill of the rain, the howling, shrieking train, the horror of being kidnapped, the disbelief at being trussed up and treated like an animal. The terrifying taxi ride, the sudden opening of the door and the appearance of a Dark Knight... the Dark Knight sleeping peacefully opposite her. She studied his face. He was dark indeed. The colour of a tree bark. Deep brown. His face was scarred. His nose was blunt and a moustache framed a wide mouth. He looked young, not more than a couple of years older than her.

Then suddenly her mind recoiled at the absence of an image!

Sanju!

The room began to spin, Sanju! Oh Sanju! Where were you! Why weren't you there? At the station. At the moment when those filthy hands lifted me away. When they kicked me like a worthless object, where were you? When they dragged me out from the train and carried away to ravage me, where was your love?

She wept, loudly, deeply, from the depths of her shattered heart. Her tears poured out as though they were the contents of the shattered organ. At that moment, along with all of Prerna's fairy tale visions of romance, was killed all of Prerna's innocence. In the course of a single night Prerna had suddenly grown up, understood the world for what it was. And most sadly, what it was not. And when she wept, she wept as much for the loss of all the wonderful, idealistic, innocent dreams that she would never again dream.

She realised she had been betrayed. By the one person around whom her entire being had existed. Suddenly she wished she'd died. What was the point now? she wondered. She wondered how she would face her parents. Despair and self-pity clutched at the hole where her heart had once been, and a loud wail issued out from her.

Mehul's eyes opened instantly at her cry. He rushed to her side, held her hand and whispered softly for her to stop crying.

In her frenzy she held onto his shirt, tugging at it, till her mind had vented out its frustration. Then as she realised she was holding onto him, she sprang back. Her shock had driven away her grief. She looked up in bewilderment at this strange ugly-attractive man from whom she could feel a soft warmth reach out to her.

He smiled at her, "So Miss Sleeping Beauty has finally woken up?"

When he smiled his face revealed a set of white and even teeth and his face seemed to radiate honesty and sincerity.

"My God! It's late, I must get home!" she said. "It's been three days since you got here," she heard him say. Stunned she turned, her hand at her mouth, stifling her scream. "What am I going to do? Who will believe me?"

She heard a steady voice say, "Try me."

It was night by the time she finished telling him her pitiful story. At the end of it, he had a thoughtful expression on his face.

"You wait here. This is the military hospital. It's about 300 km from your town. I got you here because there was no place else I knew of where I could take you. I'll go to your town and speak to your family."

She looked up in surprise at him. She could understand him, a naval officer being quick to make out a kidnap in progress and rescue her, the hostage. She could also accept that as a concerned citizen, he had her admitted to the hospital and cared for her over three days. But this last statement of his took her completely by surprise.

Why should he take on the responsibility of speaking to her parents? Why should he believe her story? Why should he continue to look at her with so much gentleness that she could feel a slight flush rising around her throat?

She imagined him talking to her parents. She wondered if they would believe him. She imagined her rather territorial brothers getting suspicious of Mehul. Maybe they would refuse to believe him, they might abuse him, hurt him. "But they won't believe you. They'll never accept me!" She cried out, concerned for him.

He held her hand gently. "Give your parents the benefit of the doubt, please."

There was a steel-like confidence in his eyes. She knew she shouldn't have doubted him. With his calmness and his quiet confidence he would convince her parents. He would handle her brothers and any trouble maker with the same ease he'd displayed in dispatching the kidnappers. He would do whatever needed to be done. That made her realise she needed to support him, discuss the details with him and arm him appropriately to cover all bases.

Mehul left immediately for her parents place. Both of them agreed they should tell only a part of the truth to her parents. The Sanju part should be kept out. They agreed that the best strategy was to tell them that she hadn't wanted to get married but wished to study and had therefore left home. The rest of the story they modified to keep out the kidnap. Merely left it at them meeting on the train and her fainting suddenly.

Partly because they were simple people and partly because of the sincerity exuded by Mehul, the family accepted the story. But her disappearance had set the town's tongues wagging and to protect her, the family decided to move and start afresh in another part of the country. Mehul was a continuing part of their family's move. He visited them often in their new home, helped them settle down, cheered Prerna and helped her decide on a career for herself. They were thick friends soon and in a few years the family had accepted him as one of their own. Then one day, during a visit, Mehul pulled Prerna aside to talk to her. He was very quiet.

"Today I met Sanju," he said to a stunned Prerna.

They talked through that night and many other nights. Mehul told Prerna about Sanju, the naval officer who had volunteered for the MARCOS unit. He spoke of his utter disregard for danger, his bravery that bordered on foolhardiness. His strange aloofness. Of his keeping away from social gatherings, of his pain and his ability to withstand it. About his uncaring nature, his defiance of death itself. His strange uncaring attitude towards himself. His desire for risk. His innate bitterness and flashes of self-loathing that emerged occasionally.

He admitted that he had grown to respect Sanju, spoke of their getting close, becoming friends, trusting each other.

He told her of Sanju's sacrifices and the kind of person he'd become. He hid nothing from her. But she realised one thing. The wounds caused by Sanju had severed her love for him once for all. She felt nothing for him. Not hate, not revenge, just nothing. She and Mehul also realised they were growing close to each other. And when he asked her, her family was relieved and she was ready.

And Sanju?

Mehul looked into her eyes. "He's the past. He'll need to accept that."

Chapter 16

She looked up. Sanju was white. All the blood had drained from his face.

Her recounting of that night, that black, dark night and the sequence of events, rendered him speechless. He could visualise the trauma that he had put her through. He had feared horrible things happened but the true extent of his actions hit home only now. All his self-loathing and self-depreciation only seemed to pale in comparison to what he had put the woman he claimed to love, through. And what if Mehul hadn't turned up that fateful night? Sanju shuddered at the thought.

So Mehul had known his story. But he had never asked. Could that be the reason that he had never asked about Sanju? As though reading his thoughts, Prerna interjected, "You see, he always knew. Both of us knew. But we had put you behind us. Long ago. We had moved on. Mehul never spoke of your actions and what you did to me that night. He was far too intelligent a person to think about a matter that didn't concern him. That judgement of you he left to me. He judged you for the man he knew, met and forged a team with. He never let our relationship cloud his with you or his judgement of you. But then neither did he try to change or influence my opinion of you. But he knew what exactly I thought of you. Because I told him of our meeting, your text messages and your despicable attempt at grabbing me."

The manner and tone with which she uttered the last sentence made Sanju flinch. "So I'm really surprised to hear his last words to you. Because if you know what I think of you and about you, you would not want to stay in the same room as me. You make me sick. If your actions that night were appalling, your pitch today is disgusting and revolting."

She paused in her quiet grief, composing her fury.

"As far as your explanation of the accident is concerned, I have a different opinion." She paused. The late evening light was very faint; the room had gone dark except for the silhouette of the two people inside. The tension was palpable. "There are murmurs all over the base about what happened that night. The event has been reconstructed by a number of experts. It is their job to know and understand human behaviour and how people react under pressure. They recreated a second by second detail of the entire rescue process. Including what happened to the people waiting for the chopper to return. It is evident that Mehul went beyond the call of his duty to return to search for you after despatching to safety the two in his custody. They also recorded the climb up the steel columns and the wait. Then they analysed the girder..."

Now the room was pitch black, they could only see each other's eyes due to the ring of the white around them. "What happened there is difficult to put down. But there was human judgement, or rather emotions, at play. There was a choice of sacrifice. And they know who made it..." They continued to look at each other unblinkingly. "A month after all this, as I was about to leave the base, I had another visitor. Someone who trained you and Mehul and knew you well."

"Cmdr. Anand," Sanju said in a cold, flat voice.

Prerna nodded, "After expressing his grief – you know how much he loved Mehul, saw him as his own son – he was leaving when I told him about the episode reconstruction. It seemed to shake him. He was silent for a long, long time. Then he spoke to me of the years when he trained you. Then he spoke of his fear of you, for you. He told me that your ability to put yourself at risk had always left him puzzled. Because unlike Mehul who had a selfless character and was brave instinctively, you were not."

"Your character analysis always portrayed you as a selfish, self-centred individual whose acts of bravery did not stem from the need for a greater good, but from the narrow perspective of a temporary suicidal tendency. This always worried him. Because you were being brave simply because you didn't care. And the big question that troubled him was what would happen when you suddenly found a reason to live. He left me with that thought. This was enough for me to reconstruct in my mind what actually happened that day on the girdle.

"I know that despite my telling you off you still harboured a fantastic notion that we would be together one day. The fact that you are here telling me about Mehul's last wish is testimony to your sick belief. Of course the one barrier to your dream in your warped mind was the presence of Mehul. Selfish as you are, you may not be evil enough to plot his death. But that night as you hung on that girdle and that girder came hurtling towards you, you consciously took the opportunity to rid yourself of the one thing you believed stood between us, by simply reverting to your self-centred nature.

"And Mehul, being Mehul, unthinkingly did what he would do. And even in his death he saw your redemption. But let me tell you one thing. I consider you to be a murderer not just of your brother and friend, but of the trust that ties people in uniform, of goodness, of sacrifice, of nobility. You are the betrayer of everything worthy in life on this planet. I'll never marry you. I loathe you. I don't wish to see you ever again in my life."

He looked at her. His eyes were strangely expressionless and still. When he spoke his voice was cracked but firm.

"Is that what you want?"

"Yes. Go away. And never ever cross my path or defile Mehul by uttering his name on your lips."

"I have nothing to say. I will never see you again, I promise."

He turned and walked away.

Chapter 17

Sanju made good his promise. If earlier he had used the memory of Prerna to remind him of his actions, now he made an all-out effort to forget her. He fought her every thought whenever it cropped up. Right from the moment he came across something that could lead to thoughts of her. He fought off thoughts of romance, love, couples. He avoided looking up at the stars, thinking back on school days, flying kites, plump little girls in spaghetti straps. He shunned thoughts of himself, of happiness, of self-loathing, of betrayal, of connections, of what people said. Of everything.

He was an automaton. A robot. Emotionless. Unflappable. Only focused on the present. Only thinking of what he was to do next. He had to wear it down. He had to win this one. He had to move forward. It was time to find himself. To know for himself what he truly was. Irrespective of the mistakes he had made. Irrespective of the reasons he was where he was. It is time, Sanju decided, to know who and what I truly am. If I ever am to leave a memory behind, let it not be one that I'm ashamed of. Let it be one in which I can redeem myself.

The terror attack caught the entire city off guard. There were four of them. They had entered the city by boat from the sea and were holed up in a 5-star hotel near Navy Nagar. The MARCOS were wired and Sanju reached the briefing room along with his unit to be addressed by a senior police commissioner.

The four terrorists had spread out through the hotel though they were pinned inside it by the police force which had completely surrounded the hotel. They were creating mayhem inside. There were over a thousand people trapped inside with them. Guests, hotel staff, attendees at the events, shoppers.... They were scouring the hotel, entering rooms, lining up people and killing them in cold blood. They had to be stopped. And fast. Sanju and three others were dropped in. Each had to take a wing.

Eyewitness accounts from the newspaper the next day:

When we heard the commotion outside, the shooting and the screams, we were terrified, and then the lights in our party hall went out. All of us lay on the ground quaking in fear and hiding from each other. It was pitch dark. There were some fifty people in the hall. Nobody spoke for what seemed like hours. Then there was silence for a long time. After which the door opened in a small crack and a thin beam of light appeared. We shook in fear; nobody had the courage to say anything. This was it. Our end. My throat went dry. But no bullets came. Instead we heard a voice whispering softly. His whispering went on for a long time. But we were terrified. Was this a trap to get us to speak up? We remained silent. The voice repeated clearly but softly, "I am from the Indian Army, please cooperate with me. I am here to help you." A few stood up, then all; we were shaking on our feet. The man entered the room silently.

His movements were swift, steady and inspired confidence. He was calm, which rubbed off on us. He arranged us in a line, one behind the other and told us to go out of the room. We hesitated. His voice rang out calmly, "Don't worry; I'm going to be at the head of the line. Any bullet that hits you will have to pass through me first." That galvanised us into action. He led us out of the room, cautiously up the two flights and out through a window, into safe hands. When the last of us had parted, he turned to go back in.

The next set of people Sanju brought out from the top floor. This one was going to be tricky because he couldn't take them along the floors below. He'd need to take them to the roof and then walk them over to the next building.

They emerged as before in a single file with Sanju at the helm. They moved quietly as possible but it was difficult to keep 20 civilians quiet. Sanju instinctively knew there was danger as they climbed to the topmost floor and neared the stairway leading to the roof. But he also knew this was a risk he had to take. Leaving the group at the head of the stairs he went ahead quietly, a split second later he threw himself down as rifle fire broke out from the corner. He shot back, killing the terrorist instantly. He stood up but a sharp pain clutched his feet. He realised he had been hit. Quickly he gathered the group and led them to the roof. They reached the edge and propped a ladder to the next building. But it was short by about 6 feet. In an inspiring move, Sanju propped his leg on the free end of the ladder and held onto the roof as the cowering group walked over him to safety.

The pain he felt was tremendous. He almost fainted in pain. A face floated into his pain-drenched mind. It was the same face that had flashed on the girdle. Mehul. The symbol of duty. A reminder of his primary responsibility.

These innocent, trapped victims. Like the man who had been strapped on his back on the girdle. Every soldier's first duty is to protect the innocent at the cost of his own life. On the girdle, in the instant the girder swung at him. He realized his primary responsibility was the man strapped to him. He therefore had to save him, putting in danger and definitely killing his best friend in the process. Mehul also knew this was right, that's why his face had flashed in his mind. That fact had established to both of them at that instant that Sanju had risen above himself and his interests to preserve the call of duty.

That message was what Mehul's eyes carried to him as he fell to almost certain death. And his redemption was in that last instruction he left for his friend. Which he believed Prerna would understand. It does not matter, thought Sanju. I understand her. I hold her no ill-will.

Weak from loss of blood, bent and broken, as the last person walked past him, his hands could no longer take the pressure and gave way.

As his body hurtled down 40 floors. Sanju wondered if he would ever be redeemed by the people who mattered.

But one man knew. Mehul knew. That was all that mattered.

Then it was all inky blackness.

Chapter 18

It's strange how places change when one returns to them after a gap of many years. But there's many a different interpretation of this statement. The first is plain and simple. The place has changed. The town has grown. Many new apartments, buildings, streets, roads, highways, malls, cinema halls, office complexes may have been added to it. And given the utter lack of town planning in India, most of this growth is utterly and absolutely chaotic. So there are more buildings on the same street. The road, instead of getting wider is made narrower thanks to the Indian habit of usurping public property for oneself. This is usually done by creating unauthorised compound walls or by extending the facade of the apartment or by creating a balcony where none existed. It is considered smart to do this: A larger apartment at the cost of traffic snarls and constant honking just outside one's door. People can put up with all kinds of trouble, noise, notices from the municipal authorities, threats from officers, bribes to get the structure authorised. All to get that extra square foot of land!

Indeed, the belief is that if one does not take it, someone else will. Hawkers and street vendors are always on the lookout for space. They begin innocuously. A vendor on foot hawking stuff from a shoulder bag. Slowly the location becomes fixed, the shoulder bag becomes a footstool that gives way to a table, it acquires a cover, a temporary shed comes up and finally a fully cemented block with an electricity connection!

Such unchecked and unauthorised growth gives the town an overcrowded, choked and changed look. Sadly no Indian city or town can claim to have improved in this change visibly, all of them only having deteriorated in direct proportion to the growth in their population.

Then there is perceptual change. A place which one leaves in one's childhood or youth looks very different when one returns to it. Houses appear smaller, lanes narrower and the mood softer. Perhaps this is a result of change in one's own physique or that the memories stored were through the senses of a small child. Whatever be the reason, places of one's childhood seem almost lost and shrunk in space-time.

And last there is the metaphorical change. Change not in the place, but in the psyche and thought process of the viewer. Half a lifetime outside a town, watching life unfold differently. An entire universe of fresh stimuli that slowly but surely widens one's perspective, forces one to reconsider reactions, gives another the benefit of viewing different more exotic options. Knowing cultural differences. The maturity of understanding the consequence of one's actions. Of a better understanding of life's realities....

All of this creates changes in the vision of the viewer. Then again, maybe long before that, the viewer changed. That is the saddest part of a return.

Sanju planned to finish the construction of the structure before the onset of the monsoon. While the belief that construction work can't take place during the monsoon is still prevalent, the truth is that technology and advancement allow construction work to actually benefit from the rain, which provides a natural curing for the freshly cemented walls and helps strengthen them.

It was not these factors that needled Sanju but the desire that the children have a home of their own at the earliest. Currently they lived in a rented place that was just not enough for them all. Moreover, the children deserved a home of their own. They crawled and ran around the limited space with such frolic that it made Sanju ache with the desire to give them a bigger place. And Sanju had to think about their future. What about their needs when it was time for school, a separate study area for each child?

He wanted his children to have all the comforts that other middle-class children in the country had. He did not want them to have any kind of inferiority complex or feel they were disadvantaged in any way. He wanted them to be bright, cheerful and positive. With this in mind he harried the contractor and pushed him to his limit. And he had to admit that he was doing it for her too. For Maya. She needed a home of her own too. Every woman wanted one. A place, no matter how large or small, with her unique signature on it.

Men were completely unlike women when it came to homes. Either they bought them and did them up to show off to their peers, or they didn't care much about their dwelling space and kept it merely at a utilitarian level.

Stocked with the bare basics, merely a place they could return to at night, equipped with just the right fittings to serve speedy arrivals and departures.

But women were different. Even as little girls they'd begin to give a unique and different look to their immediate space, be it their rooms, cubicles in office, desks at school... any space they call their own. And every woman's space differs from another's, not in a broad sense – most men wouldn't pick up on the subtle differences – but in the finer details. And while they may appreciate another's design, if they were to take over the same space they would initiate tiny changes in the detail till over time the space looked entirely different.

Sisters make sure they're different from each other, daughters from mothers and aunts and even the best of friends. And every woman deserved a home of her own, which she could do up completely as she wished. In fact, when a woman enters her home for the first time, however raw and unfinished it may be, a dreamy look enters her eyes.The look persists as she passes through each room, feels every wall, takes in the environment and lets delight and warmth spread from her heart to the rest of her person. She may twirl, smile, laugh and if the man is lucky enough bestow him with some heartfelt kisses, enough for him to forget the huge loan he took to make her dream come true. A few minutes later, her senses assuaged, more practical thoughts begin entering her head. Things she needs changed, appliances, the needs of her children; and along with these thoughts come those long-suppressed wishes stored in the hidden recesses of her mind since childhood for her unique home.

And ruthlessly she goes about getting this done. Men beware! No suggestions are welcome, no barrier big enough. Nothing can stop a woman whose home is ready to bear her stamp. And Maya deserved a place where she could leave her stamp. Not that she'd ever asked or even hinted but he felt for her and knew that as a woman, she would love to have a place of her own. And he was determined to give her and the kids that space well before the monsoon arrived.

The contractor at the site saw Sanju approach and warned his people to double up. He was nervous himself. These military types missed nothing and could not be messed with. But given that he had learnt his lesson the hard way and Sanju had cracked the whip so often to bring them into line, he and his people were well on schedule. Sanju came up and addressed him. They knew the drill. Silently he took Sanju over the site and gave him a to-the-point update. For all their efforts, Sanju managed to point out three areas that he had missed completing as per the schedule. Cursing the supervisor under his breath the contactor agreed to put in extra time to finish those. Sanju left with a single sentence. This was enough to send a chill down the contractor's spine.

Once Sanju had gone he hunted out the supervisor who was taking a smoke break and admonished him severely. This supervisor was new and careless. He turned to the contractor and said contemptuously, "*Arrey itna kyun darte ho*? That fellow is blind and lame and this is a bloody orphanage for wretched kids run by that shameless woman!"

Before he knew it, he was beaten to the ground by the contractor. "First, don't you call him that...," the contractor's voice had a menacing ring to it. "He's a legend, a hero. From this little town. He's our pride. And most important, he's taught us what no man ever has before.

That even after losing everything you can contribute and be useful to society. Each of those 100 children would have been dead or sold into child labour had Sanju not rescued them. He took on the most powerful and dangerous mafia in this region. He is threatened and harried every day. Yet he shows no fear. He has inspired bravery in all of us and today our entire town is far more courageous in tackling crime and standing up to such mafia."

Then his voice took on a different scornful tone. "What have you done in your life? You are lazy and have to be pushed hard to do work that you promised to do. Then you go home every evening drunk and beat your wife. It's ridiculous that a pathetic scum-bag like you can speak like this about such a fine woman. If you ever use such language about her again that will be end of you and I'll personally wring your neck. She is the person who nursed him back to health. Who helped him recover physically and mentally. What happened to her is not her fault. The mentally sick and diseased men in this place can do the same to any of our women too. But she was not cowed by them nor did she give up on life. She has inspired us with her bravery and won our respect by re-creating Sanju. She is the quiet force behind him. The children are our future and what we are building here is hope."

Chapter 19

He was not dead. But it was worse. He was floating in a space between life and death. Immersed in a sea of red hot, molten lava, dipped in salt, pepper and vinegar, tormented with a million pinpoints of pain. Some of those pins tore deep into his muscle, going deeper and drilling through his bones, then exploding with a million times the pressure of a dentist wrenching out a molar without anaesthesia. His skin was burning; he was on a spit being roasted alive, like a pathetic chicken being cooked in a highway 'tandoor'. Only, he was alive. He could feel the flesh on his arms and legs turn red and raw. He could see the pink flesh turn deep red. He saw the still and coagulated blood in his veins. He screamed in gut-wrenching pain. Now his flesh was overcooked, it began to drop off his skeleton, he could see his bones. The raging fire cooked the fat on the bone. It sizzled as he watched in horror, nauseated by the sound. His throat had gone dry and he gasped as he struggled to scream. He wept but that made him realise he had no tears to let out. His eyes had turned dry in the raging heat of the flames and soon began burning. They burnt as though they were fireballs that soon grew into a nuclear fissure. He could smell the rotting at its core as though his eyes were evaporating, cell by cell.

There was nowhere he could go. Nothing, it appeared, could give him refuge. His mind, body and soul cried for relief, for some rest. He desperately wanted to sink into sleep... of any kind. But the pain was like a noose, reining him in. Till he was exhausted, defeated and thirsting for liberation.

"Is there no end to my suffering?" he screamed to an endless red burning world, which seemed not to hear or care. It was a throbbing, evil universe, with no heart or feeling. Like the innards of a nuclear reactor. It only knew how to cook and convert a being into its lowest form. Sanju wept and cried for death. He would have given anything for the merciful relief of the end of it all. If ever there was hell, if ever there was suffering, if ever there was a price to be paid for one's actions, then Sanju was enduring it all. But even this pain had to pass. Slowly Sanju's sanity began to return. His mind regained control of his conscious being. He returned from the fiery innards of hell to his hospital bed. His pain became less metaphysical and more relatable.

The first few months were a whirl. He had no idea when he gained consciousness and encountered darkness for the first time. It was just bits of time. Seconds in which his mind would surface from the depth of a comfortable coma before returning to it. Then the intervals of consciousness increased. Sometimes the pain woke him up. He was unable to move, he realised, and his body was racked with pain. It shot through his body and he would scream out. But this pain was unlike the earlier pain of punishment. This was the pain of healing. Ending each time with a soft sweet tinge of feeling. Slowly he became aware of movement and talk around him. His movements would alert the voices and he would feel a pin prick before returning to the calmness of the coma.

His body healed. He was young and extremely fit, which helped. His back, arms, ribs, skull, legs were set, or replaced with metal, plastic or silicone. Nerves were reconnected. Blood vessels cut and transplanted. Bit by bit his body was reconstructed. But like anything that is smashed to bits it was impossible to restore it to its original shape.

Much like a broken doll of clay glued together, so was Sanju put together by the skill and adhesiveness of science and his own physical strength. However he would never again be the same Sanju. That Sanju died with the fall. And despite their best efforts, the military doctors could not save his sight or his left leg, which had been literally blown apart by the gun shot and the subsequent fall. The prosthetic leg in its place ensured he could walk, without the use of crutches but with a limp. The fall had disturbed the part of his brain that controlled vision due to which he could not see anything though his eyes were in near perfect condition. He was eventually discharged from the hospital. He was sitting on his bed, helplessly waiting for assistance to get to the naval base, when he felt a presence in his hospital room. As he adapted to his new dark world, he had begun to rely more on his other senses, including the sixth. His senses told him the diffident visitor was not from the hospital staff.

The smell of crispness and the Navy was there, though, but Sanju realised this was not his naval escort who'd have clicked his heels and announced himself.

"Yes?"

"It's me, Sanju..."

Sanju smiled and leapt to his feet in joy, "Cmdr. Anand Sir!"

In his excitement, he forgot all about his blindness and crashed into the bedpost and a medical desk. He slipped but Anand held him.

"Easy boy.... I offered to take you back to the base and the Admiral agreed."

"Sir, you needn't have... the staff would have been..."

"No, Sanju... there has been something on my mind for many years now, which I had to clear with you..." "Sanju waited quietly. The older man cleared his throat and began speaking.

"Ever since your academy and training days, I have always doubted you."

Sanju began to protest but Anand cut him short. "No, let me speak. I need to clear the air and my heart. I always doubted your motivation for doing what you did. To me it stemmed from self-destruction rather than compassion."

"Which drove Mehul..." Sanju interjected.

Anand shot him a keen look before continuing, "Yes, that is right. I felt you were driven by a desire to seek death, which others saw as fearlessness. It was merely the lack of a desire to live. I always asked myself, what if you found one suddenly? Then the next time you wouldn't seek death. Were you brave enough to put yourself ahead of others as is required of a naval officer or would you preserve yourself? Mehul was like a son to me and confided in me after his marriage the whole sordid story of the three of you. He told me because there was no one else he could speak to. You know my wife Shraddha and I are childless. Mehul was the son we never had. When I heard of his death I lost my sense of reason and I blamed you for his death. My fears about you told me that you had, in desire for his wife, passed death to him, which was yours to stand in for. So sure was I that I hinted the same to Prerna when I met her.

"I'm here, my son, to ask for your forgiveness. Because my love for Mehul and my deep suspicion of you clouded my judgement of you, a fine man and officer. What you did during the terrorist attack was sacrifice of the highest order, which stemmed from pure bravery and compassion. I was called in by Admiral Nair who reminded me of the night at the girdle and underscored the point that the survivor was strapped on your back. He told me that had he been in your place he'd have done exactly what you did. So would Mehul, had your positions been interchanged.

"I know that Prerna met you and spoke to you harshly. If that led to you sacrificing yourself at the altar of duty to prove your innocence then I am completely to blame for your current predicament. I am willing to accept any punishment you deem right for me. But please accept my apology."

Sanju could hold out no longer.

"Please, Sir, don't shame me. What you said is true partly and therefore your assessment is logical. You were right when you said that my bravery stemmed initially from the desire for death. But all that changed when I met Mehul. His character and appeal made me find a better man in myself. You are right that I misbehaved with Prerna. I held thoughts for my brother's wife not becoming of a naval officer. I was blind in my love. It's true that I indeed wished Mehul wasn't there because I felt his absence would make it easier for me to claim Prerna for my own. But my respect and duty never wavered and when Mehul returned to rescue me from the fire I had made up my mind to move out of this base to another. I only wished the survivor had been strapped to Mehul so all this tragedy would have ended that night. I really was the odd one out.

"I went to meet Prerna to tell her about Mehul's last words only so that she would know that he saw things differently. Most important, I was going to tell her that despite what Mehul said I was going away and could never touch her or see her in any light other than as my brother's wife.

"But she had a different perspective. Though I realised the end point was the same – my going away for good. So I thought to myself, why bother with clarification? Let her continue to hate me. I deserved it for what I'd done to her. Let her live with hate in her heart for me."

Chapter 20

Sanju's happiest moment came when one day the door of his naval quarters opened to reveal his estranged family. His father, mother, sister and her family – a husband and little daughter. At his father's insistence Sanju agreed to return to the town he grew up in. His father had retired from the bank and worked for a private company that was deep into philanthropic activities. When they heard of Sanju's desire to set up an orphanage in his home town in memory of Mehul, his family was elated. His father helped him prepare the business plan and present the case to the company, who agreed to help Sanju.

Sanju was clear that the orphanage would shelter children from all sections of society. But to create an ecosystem where such children were identified, located, picked up and nurtured was a task to challenge any human being and Sanju with his disability and vision impairment found it difficult even to do simple small tasks. His desire to do something for society hit a wall and Sanju found himself frustrated and depressed.

As he sat one day, bitterly cursing his life, his sister entered the room and she was not alone.

"This is Maya." she said simply, "Maya is trained to help the vision impaired find their way without help. Now Sanju, it is up to you to be patient, determined and strong and let Maya help you."

The first thing he realised was that Maya rarely spoke. She used touch to convey meaning. As Sanju figured his way about his dark world, he realised how much the sense of sight had overridden the sense of touch. Under Maya's expert guidance he began to *feel* *h*is way around the world. He was a fast learner, eager to try with a positive attitude and Maya was a patient, indefatigable teacher. Together they progressed fast. Since work required that Sanju travel around to meet and create the ecosystem, Maya began to accompany him. Slowly she was drawn to his work and the noble objective behind it. She was affected by the infectious enthusiasm that Sanju brought to every day. She slowly began to dream his dream.

Sanju often wondered about Maya and who she was. She never volunteered any information about herself and Sanju was too much the chivalrous naval officer to ask. And how did it matter who she was, what her background was or how she looked? Thought Sanju.

What mattered was the sweetness in her nature, the kindness in her soul and the willingness in her to contribute to a greater societal good. Yet he often wondered about her. The way she moved, the rare sounds she made when she moved around the house, the sound of her laughter – so musical and so enlivening. All of this had created a picture of her in his mind. A picture of a very sensitive person, with lovely expressive eyes and a soft, natural glow on her face, someone whose loveliness, radiance and inherent niceness brought out the best in other people.

He knew her hands were well shaped, though her palms were rough indicating that she did a lot of housework. Was she married? Was she in love with somebody else?

He told himself that he must proceed carefully. She rarely spoke. Why? Was it a disability? Or had she been traumatized so terribly that she'd lost her voice? Or was she just too shy to speak? The last he disregarded because it was more than a year that he'd known her and no normal person would have been quiet for so long out of shyness. But he had to know. Rather than ask her he decided to ask his sister.

"Ha ha, Sanju, what do you want to know about Maya? No, she is not married. Nor does she have a boyfriend. Yes, she's from a good family but they live in another state. Is she beautiful? Of course she is; gentle, intelligent and beautiful."

Then her voice took on a serious note, "Sanju bhaiyya, I don't know why you are asking these questions. If it is mere curiosity it is fine but if you're getting serious about her then there are some things you must know, which will tell you what the poor girl has been through.

"A few years back Maya, a bright young postgraduate, worked at a local NGO. She studied in JNU Delhi and has a master's degree in sociology. With dreams of making a significant change in society and helping the under-privileged, especially children, this daughter of a senior bureaucrat set up base in our town. She got wind of a human trafficking racket. She investigated it and with the help of the local police exposed some very powerful people who were subsequently punished in a high-profile verdict. The family of those powerful people swore revenge on her.

Despite warnings she refused to take police protection and continued with her job. One day her co-worker came rushing into town. He had been badly beaten and she had been kidnapped.

A huge dragnet was laid as the entire town searched for her. It was more than three days later that they found her. What those people had done cannot be described, but it left her shell-shocked and withdrawn. It took a couple of years for her to recover. She decided to fight her demons and show those people that they had not beaten her and that's why she's here."

Sanju could feel Maya's presence in the room although his sister couldn't. He said, "Maya I'll get you justice. I promise you I will bring your attackers to book."

In that moment something happened. Something like the discovery of a new universe. Is this what philosophers call catharsis? Was that the moment when Sanju turned the corner and became a new soul? When does a man finally conquer his insecurities and failures to emerge a hero?

Maya came back to life with those words. It did not matter to her that Sanju was blind and crippled. It did not enter her mind to question how he would make good his promise. She didn't really care if she lived or died after hearing his words. For though she had heard words of sympathy, words of encouragement and words of support, no one had offered to get her justice. She was honest enough to admit that none was possible in view of the people involved. But here was a man. Whose honest voice and clear intent had offered what her heart was bleeding for: someone to wipe her tears and fight for her. The event was not important, the reason was not important, the end result too was not important. What mattered was that her feelings mattered to someone. That a man felt for

114

her, understood her, took responsibility for her and with sincere intent made his objective the delivering of justice to her.

Maya had always been a capable independent woman who knew what she wanted in life. Her family in the city was well off and had ensured the best education for her. She was bright, focused and intent on making a difference to society. She believed it was her duty to help the underprivileged. She had believed that her fight against the trafficking of women would be supported by the town authorities. But she'd been horribly wrong. Nobody helped her, supported her or offered to take up her fight. Till Sanju.

In the mid-morning glow, the sound of the little girls laughing and giggling seemed perfectly matched with the bright yellow light and crisp green surrounding. The early November nip and the benign sun seemed to perfectly balance each other on the mercury scale. Maya felt warmth spread through her as she quickened her pace to walk through the school's structure. She was already smiling to herself when she turned the corner to see the girls sitting around Sanju in a tight circle. She managed to hold back her own giggle as she heard him imitate her. He's quite good at it, she thought to herself. She was surprised to see the detail with which he was mimicking her much to the amusement of the pack of little girls. She held back and observed them unseen. She'd known him for close to two years now and always as a man who never spoke more than he needed to. Not that he was rude or snobbish, on the contrary he was always gentle and respectful. Sometimes his voice was so low it seemed little more than a whisper. But it was always clear and firm. He seemed genuinely concerned about her and on the occasions their work stretched late, he'd accompany her home, albeit silently.

Never in the two years had he ever enquired about her background or asked for any details about her life. He seemed to respect her for her work, seeking her advice often, trusting her judgement of people and finance and always acknowledging her effort as being critical to the progress they were making.

"He knows what happened to me," she thought. After all, what happened to her was in the public domain. Moreover this was small-town India, where even small matters were amplified out of proportion. And her case was hardly a small matter. She wondered what else he had been told about her; certain that some of it couldn't have been good judging by the way some townspeople treated her. Most citizens were polite. "But they may not necessarily be nice in what they say of me...," she thought, feeling depressed. She had trained herself to remain unaffected by gossip, choosing to remain alone and immerse herself in the activities of the orphanage.

"Did it matter what he knew, how much of the truth it was and what he thought of her?" she sighed. "Yes," she heard herself say grudgingly. He was the only man who made her feel valued. "Somehow we are similar," she mused. "He's rarely spoken about himself too." He kept away from social gatherings and shunned public attention. But then again, she knew most things about him, courtesy the gossip mills of small-time India. He was a product of this town, a brave officer whose courageous actions were etched in the front pages of the national newspapers. The example that would forever be given to young cadets from the NDA and IMA, of the honour in putting oneself in the line of fire ahead of civilians.

It was the clarity of his thinking, the righteousness in his resolve, the calmness in his tenacity that she found so attractive about him. The quiet dedication with which he had set about building this orphanage with his disability pension told the story of a man carrying a weight on his shoulders. Silent but firm, handicapped but resolute, disadvantaged but determined he seemed always the man standing quietly in the shadows. The only time he came to life was when he was interacting with the children. He seemed a transformed man as he laughed with them. The sunlight fell directly on his face and torso. Then one little girl said something to him and a broad smile creased his face. At that moment, as he threw back his head and laughed from his heart, something seemed to melt in that broken, ravaged face. The sunlight suddenly highlighted the strong and square lines of his face against the deep shadow of his neck, the smile softened the scars that crisscrossed his face and she momentarily caught a glimpse of a hauntingly handsome man... the man he once must have been. Then suddenly he turned his head to look directly at her, forcing her involuntarily to take a step back. He was still smiling as he looked at her, the warmth of the moment glowing in his sightless eyes.

Chapter 21

A series of strange incidents was picked up initially by local papers and then by the mainline dailies about happenings around the town. Human trafficking instances were being brought to light with regularity. What was astounding was the manner in which these were coming to light. These were not reports of the occurrences of human trafficking. No report talked about missing children from homes, or about parents or police searching these children. This was something else.

A vigilante was on the loose.

Somebody who had decided to target those who trafficked in humans. Somebody who knew how, where and when they operated. Someone who kept many steps ahead of them. Somebody who had taken it upon himself to purge society of these vermin. And that somebody was going about the task with ruthless, cold and absolute precision.

There was no mercy shown to the perpetrators of the crime. There were no questions asked, no answers given. Almost as if a bunch of ghosts had descended on the region. Like howling banshees they went about, butchering and killing the gang members. No attempt would be made to rehabilitate the victims. No conversations would take place. But after every attack, a terse message would be received by the inspector of police of the closest chowki.

A truck would be found with kidnapped people in it. Villagers from nearly areas would report foiled kidnapping attempts with the hunters becoming the hunted as they tried to carry away poor villagers. All this led to speculation and talk. The state as well as the central government woke up to some realities:

- That the district had been both a source and transit point for human trafficking.
- That these activities had been on for quite some time right under the nose of the authorities and despite complaints and reports by local papers and NGO's no action had been taken. Even when a girl reporting this had been kidnapped and tortured.
- That now the hunters had become the hunted and somebody or some group was systematically attacking and finishing the traffickers. The trafficker's logistics had been destroyed. Their sourcing had been nipped. The entire area had become too hot for them to use as a transit point. Their key operators in the area had been isolated and were on the run.

The centre cracked the whip and the CBI was pressed into the investigation. In a few months the entire trafficking ring was busted from the source point and from the transit perspective. Local MLAs were found to be hand-in-glove with the ring leaders. Under the full glare of the media no one could escape the falling axe and the repercussions of a baying-for-blood public.

Heads rolled in the administration system and the police force as people's rage spilt forth. The gang was completely busted and the news attracted western attention and UNESCO involvement. A series of studies was carried out, the entire administration was uprooted and a new system took its place in the town and district and a year later there was no trace of the gang or the people who backed them.

Yet one question remained unanswered. Who hit them initially and exposed them? The precision and timing and surgical skill with which it was done signalled a professional force. Speculation was rife. Popular theories were:

- That this was done by a rival international group whom this gang had rubbed the wrong way and who were hell bent on destroying the traffickers completely.
- This was done by the central police. Yet given that that organisation too was riddled with informers it was found strange that no leaks occurred.

The political supporters and local goons who were hand in glove with the villains also received punishment. Many were found paralysed in body or spirit after having been kidnapped and kept hidden for days. None of these people were ever the same again. The kind of physical and mental torture they were put through rendered them mentally unstable and shadows of their former selves. Given that their reign was a result of their stature and mental alacrity, their reduced condition left them lonely, without their fawning selfish supporters and without power and support they lost everything, ending up destitute.

Whatever the theories, the truth was never known. Once the back of organised crime was broken, there was no record of any other gang in the vicinity or mention of any more attacks. The hunters disappeared into the darkness as quietly as they had come. Only the villagers sometimes spoke of dark men in beards with their faces covered, appearing and disappearing in the dark. Leading to speculation of ghosts and spirits of the dead wreaking revenge. Given the superstitious nature and low level of education, this theory took firm root and soon people were terrified to be associated with anyone remotely linked to the traffickers.

It was difficult for Singh to find shelter. He was the last of the ring leaders of the gang. There had been four of them. But in the last month he had found each of his three companions brutally murdered. They had been cut and bled slowly, tortured like a sacrifice, and finally skinned alive and left to die. The very thought of their death made him shiver. His mind leapt to the tales he'd heard of a supernatural being stalking them and he shivered. But he was a vicious cruel man who didn't fear anything. He kept his gun and knife handy. He was waiting for things to die down before starting again. Now he was hiding in a hut in a remote hamlet in the forest. He awoke with a start. Someone was whispering his name outside. He reached for his gun quietly.

Trap!

The gun was in a steel wire which snapped around his wrist. He was pulled through the roof and thrown on the ground. It was pitch dark. Singh wet his pants in fear. He moaned. He opened his eyes. He could make out a shape in front of him. A torch came on and he recognised the girl instantly! She was the one he and the other three had raped and mutilated. She was looking at him with quiet rage in her eyes. But he grew confident. This woman! I'll kill her!

He lunged at her but received a kick on his back that sent him sprawling. He turned and recognised the man who had kicked him. It was the blind, crippled navy officer.

Why! Singh thought, First I'll kill him and take her again. But the woman smiled, rage and anger in her smile! She switched off the torch and it was inky blackness.

Then the man spoke. "We're even now."

Singh could almost feel the mocking smile in his opponent's voice. A nameless terror clutched at his throat. In his mind, flashes of his various crimes zoomed in and out till his thoughts were in a choked whirl. The whirling reached a crescendo as he feebly tried to get up and run. His eyes bulged with fear. The icy cold voice cut through the chilly winter air, "Singh you will be in hell with your evil mates. But it will be a long and painful road for you..."

Chapter 22

The sun was setting. It was a beautiful evening and the winter chill was cosy yet. Sanju shook the hand of the older man as he prepared to leave.

"Thank you, Cmdr. Anand, for this."

Both men burst out laughing. "From the look of it we should be doing this more often," Anand said.

Exactly three months earlier, Commander Anand had received a phone call from one of his finest students.

It had taken 15 minutes for Sanju to explain the situation to Anand. The town and the adjoining tribal area, the organised gang of human traffickers who operated with impunity in those regions. The powerful people behind it. The unstated support they received from those in power. The impotence of the local authorities to curb the crime. The spill-over effect of the crime on the morale of the town.

But he didn't tell him about Maya. All he told him was about the incident. He told him about the need to end the problem and eradicate the evil from the region. With his goodwill and Maya's knowledge of the trade, they were able to piece together the entire modus operandi of the gang. The gang had become careless and worked without taking much cover. Most of the people involved had begun to shoot their mouths off at local bars and drinking joints. Quickly Sanju mapped the entire operational area of the gang, their travel routes, their exchange points, their transit regions; who their supporters were, the kingpin, the hatchet men and the fringe staff. An entire network of people, places, roads, junctions and stop points had been worked out by him down to the last detail. Now he needed a hammer to strike the blows. And blood ran thicker than anything else. This was the blood of a band of brothers united by the highest cause.

So when Sanju picked up the phone and called his ex-CO, Anand was more than willing to help.

Anand said, "While the armed forces are geared to defend the country from external threat, clearly our greater problem is internal. Especially with a ruling class who seem incapable of leading us anywhere. As far as these vermin are concerned, it was an exercise for the boys lest they lose touch. And they needed no motivation. When they heard it was for you and especially who were to be eliminated there was a queue outside my house. You won't believe it but the final team was chosen by a draw of lots!

"There is still a huge waiting list so just call us if you need anything to be done. Believe me, even if you take up this task for the whole country you will not fall short of volunteers!"

Both men had a hearty laugh.

"Well, see you around then, Sanju. Do drop in to meet me and Shraddha when you can and the boys too."

"I surely will, once things settle a bit." Cmdr. Anand hopped into the waiting car. He was very thoughtful. *There is still something I have to do for Sanju,* he thought to himself. He picked up his phone and called his PA. "Ramesh, can you slot me for a day trip to Pune next week?"

Sanju turned back and entered his home. His sister was down for the weekend and he looked forward to spending the evening with her. "Sanju bhaiyya, I'm so proud of you."

He chuckled, "Arrey what have I done?"

"C'mon bhaiyya, you can fool everyone but not me! I know what you have done for the town. But most importantly for Maya. You have no idea how much this means to her. You have liberated her. She's a new woman now. She smiles and talks! She's transformed you know. And…"

Sanju's smile widened, "Yes… and?"

His sister's voice now had a note of hesitation. "She's really drawn to you bhaiyya… you don't know the way her eyes light up when she sees you… the way she perks up and smiles when people talk about you. She has asked me so much about you. She really likes you a lot."

She said the last sentence with so much of intensity and feeling that Sanju turned sharply to her. He said quietly, "Deeps, she's making a mistake…. Look at me. I'm not even a full man. I'm a cripple Deeps. I've been broken in so many parts. I don't even know if I can be a man…"

He spoke softly to let the significance of his last sentence sink in.

"I think Maya's a beautiful and lovely woman. She is pure in her heart and soul. What happened to her was not her fault. She is kind and gentle and caring. Everything about her is genuine. Her husband will be a very lucky man. His life will be blessed. But she deserves better than me…"

"But what if I love you?"

Sanju whirled around to where Maya stood on his doorstep, tears of happiness rolling down her radiant, glowing face.

Chapter 23

The orphanage was ready. The school adjacent to it was being given a last coat of paint. Sanju was really happy. He looked forward to the day when the children would move in.

But there was an additional spring in his step as he walked beyond the small wall that separated the compound housing the school and the orphanage, through the tiny wicker-gate that was the break in the wall into the next compound where the cottage was being given its finishing touches.

He could feel the smile on his face as he pushed open the main door and entered it.

The furniture, sparse as it was, was in place. The kitchen was ready. The study had its contents, albeit in cardboard boxes. They needed to be emptied onto the shelves waiting patiently on the walls. The tiny staircase led to three bedrooms and further on, to the attic.

The bougainvillea over the years should cover the cottage well, he thought dreamily, to give it the look he always wanted for his home. But he'd never see it. He smiled again. Who cares? I'll be happy... like now, I'm standing at the window and can't see a thing but I'm happy to just be here.

He smelt her.

"Prerna?" Surprise and shock in his voice.

She came rushing to him and hugged him. She began sobbing on his shoulder.

"I'm so sorry, Sanju, really so sorry. I said and thought such horrible things of you. I've hurt you, maligned you and treated you so badly. I never gave you a chance to speak. I judged you and damned you without a thought."

Sanju was still in shock. His arms were frozen in position inches above her shoulder. From force of habit, he slowly embraced her. That feel. That familiar feel. Memories came rushing back.

The girl in the spaghetti straps. The moment he fell in love with her. His lonely nights consumed in her memory. Her doting love. Her dash to him on the day she was to be betrothed.

Then other more painful memories engulfed him. His ditching of her. Meeting her again. Mehul. The rigs. The final meeting. The promise he made.

He stepped back and asked her softly, "Cmdr. Anand?"

Prerna wiped her tears and composed herself. "Yes, he told me everything. What actually happened that night on the girder. About you and Mehul. About your view on it. How you merely wanted to tell me without any selfish motive. He told me how you saved people from the terrorists during the attack. How you sacrificed your everything, how much you suffered subsequently. How you lost vision, your limb, yet your positivity about life did not change. How honourably you've acquitted yourself here. How you are making a difference to people. How you've brought hope and love to the life of people around. How much you've grown as a human."

Sanju was silent.

He felt a deep sigh in his heart. Finally he knew he had forgiven himself. It was like a load off his mind. What we do returns to haunt us in life; we cannot escape it or run away. Responsibility needs to be taken up when it is meant to be. Facing up to choices and taking responsibility for actions is perhaps the only way to absolve oneself of wrong done. But there was still something rankling in him. He had to know from her. Only then would his soul find peace.

They both sat down on the sofa. He held her hands in his. "Despite all this there is still something that I never managed to say to you. Which I should have."

"I'm sorry, Prerna. Sorry for breaking your heart. For ditching you on the most important day of our life. For leaving you in a situation that put you at high risk and could have ruined your life. I'm sorry for behaving like a boor. For attempting to win you back when you were my brother's wife. I behaved badly and I deserved what I got."

He could feel Prerna smile and shake her head.

"Actually no. You shouldn't feel sorry. Because indirectly you gave me the most important person in my life. Mehul. Had you turned up, I would never have met the person I grew to love. When I look back, I realise that what I felt for you was infatuation. But from Mehul I learnt what it is to love, to earn love. Even though our life together was short it was rich and fulfilling. I knew his profession and knew how much his duty and country mattered to him so mentally I was prepared for a life in which he was no more. Because I valued more the fullness of the life, however short, that I shared with him."

A weight lifted off both their shoulders.

"This conversation between us has been due for eons. And now we can resume our respective lives. I leave for Pune tonight, but do keep in touch." Prerna looked up and into his eyes. His blind, sightless eyes. He could feel her looking at him. "I'm not much of a man any more, Prerna" he said ruefully. "I'm not the Sanju you knew and loved. I've lost everything I had, then found it too. Sometimes I feel glad that it happened to me. I believe I lost the worst parts of me and gained something in turn that's so beautiful that it compensates all that I lost."

"Am I a part of that which you're glad to have lost?" Prerna asked searchingly.

"Oh no, never, Prerna, I am nothing if not for you. You created me. Made me. What would I have been had you not been there in my life? A lonely cloud. Traversing the dark night. Unwept, unknown, uncared for and unlamented. You gave my life direction, purpose, forced me to see myself, seek myself out and then redeem myself. You will always remain in my heart."

They got up and embraced each other. Time stood still as they relived every moment of their lives together. A door slamming shut broke their reverie.

"Best of luck."

Sanju returned home, thoughtful but liberated. Was there something else he was feeling?

Was he feeling a sense of loss?

Then another image entered his mind. Maya. A feeling of elation ran through him.

He was free! Finally free! The skies looked bright and clear. He wanted to scream wildly and throw himself into the icy waters of some lake. He had been dead. He was born anew. He felt himself come to life. He was a man again. He had a heart. He could live and love again. He saw her running towards him in his mind.

Maya. Prerna. His mind stopped as if stunned.

Suddenly he heard running feet reach him. "What did you say to her, Sanju? What did you tell her?"

"Who? What have I said?" Sanju asked, completely bewildered.

"Maya, Sanju, What did you tell her? What happened? She came with tears pouring from her eyes. She said just one sentence. 'Sanju should be happy now. He's got what he always wanted.' She left immediately. It appears she has left home."

"No Deepa! No no! Did she come to the school?" he asked her.

"Yes, she went there searching for you. She returned almost instantly. Why, what happened?"

Sanju shook his head in disbelief, "Prerna came to visit me," he said hollowly. "She said she had forgiven me. We spoke a lot and we embraced. This could have been misconstrued by Maya." He shook his head and seemed to go hollow as he thought of fate's cruellest twist. "Where did she say she was going?" Sanju gripped her tight.

"No one knows. Oh Sanju! Sanju!" Deepa hugged her brother and began to cry for him and for the world he had just lost.

Again.

Chapter 24

As flying became the preferred choice of travel for middle-class India, airports began sprouting up in tier two towns, making hitherto 'distant' regions reachable within half a day from any major city. The airport on the outskirts of the nearby city was about two-and-a-half hours from Sanju's town, making air travel accessible and attractive to the town's middle class and wealthy population.

The airport was small but built by a private company with vision that had given it an all-glass, open architectural feel. It had space for a small shopping mall and a food court, a standalone restaurant and a couple of coffee shops. The airport was empty at that hour. Flights were limited since the airport was still considered a feeder route for flights en route to a larger hub. Passenger traffic peaked during some days of the month and remained erratic on others. An empty airport has a strangely calm feel to it. Almost like a temple in the afternoon when the presiding deity had retired for a siesta. The late afternoon sun cast lazy shadows through the huge glass panels that made up the facade. The departure lounge had a sprinkling of people, most dozing in its comfortable environment.

Two women sitting in the lounge were the only people who appeared to be in some state of wakefulness, but each appeared too deep in her own thoughts to notice the other. A casual observer would have sworn that the two women were alike, for at a glance there was striking similarity between them. They were about the same age, extremely attractive and carried themselves with a certain aura of self-assurance, poise and grace. They seemed well educated and from good backgrounds. Their appearance, though different, was such that had one of them not been too lost in thought to pay attention to the other she would have instantly approved the other's attire for colour, combination, cut and design. Perhaps had they met under different circumstances they may have bonded well and become good friends. Had life thrown them together at some earlier point in their lives, they may have shared a deeper understanding and earned each other's respect.

But at that moment it was evident even to a casual viewer that both women were under severe personal stress. Both appeared to be maintaining their composure with great difficulty. Their eyes, puffy at the edges, red rimmed and showing signs of eye-liner smear, indicated that both had recently been crying and were in distress.

But no observer could have guessed that at the epicentre of the storm currently raging in the minds of both women was the same man. Both would have been stunned to know that they loved the same man. Each believed she had just left him free for another woman, she believed was more deserving. Neither knew that the woman for whom she'd thrown away her dream was sitting across her with the very same thoughts coursing through her mind.

The public announcement system came to life and a soothing voice informed the sparse audience that their flight had been delayed by an hour. Neither woman seemed particularly affected by this announcement. Some part of them perhaps wished to delay their departure and was glad at the news. Slowly they made their way to the restroom, where for a brief instant their eyes met in the huge mirror and for the first time they became aware of the physical presence of the other. After leaving the restroom one walked to the bookstore and dispiritedly rummaged through the magazines before making her way to the coffee shop. As she dropped onto the couch, she felt someone approach. She looked up to catch sight of the woman she had seen only minutes earlier in the restroom, take the opposite seat. "Sorry, didn't know this was taken." She rose to leave when the other stopped her.

"It's okay, there's no one coming there," the other clarified with a wan smile.

The words seemed loaded and she felt it strike a chord deep inside her as she slowly sat back. The smile on her lips was part bitter, part rueful as she repeated the statement, "No one coming... how true!"

The words came out from her mouth involuntarily. The other woman looked up as she heard them and said, "I wondered if there could be someone else as lost as I am..."

"Try me!"

"I've lost my heart... forever, it appears."

"I've lost mine too but now I wonder if I had it at all in the first place!"

"Why did I lose it? Was it my fault? Was I too quick in making a judgement?"

"Maybe I should have waited before deciding."

"I should never have gone that way. It got me nothing but pain."

They smiled weakly at each other. A sisterly smile; as they began to understand the similarity of their situations.

The thought, like a burst of bright sunlight, seemed to lighten the mood and for the first time they smiled at each other and began a conversation that would change the course of their lives forever.

"Why do we women take things so much to our hearts? Why do we deliberate and agonise so much in matters of love? Is it that we are insecure and only on the lookout for things that make us unhappy? Why can't we take things at face value, be practical about things and move on?"

The other woman leaned forward, nodding in agreement with the stranger opposite. "Maybe we want more. We aren't content with what we see. We look for 'what ifs'. I wonder if we are ever content with anything."

"So unlike men," the first one sighed. "They get married without necessarily worrying about love."

"Or walk out of a marriage for love."

Both women paused to think and reflect on their lives in the context of what they had just said. Realisation dawned on them simultaneously and both gently shook their heads as though they'd found a possible direction to follow.

"I think we could be judging them too harshly."

"Yes. Or maybe it's we who are not ready yet."

They looked at each other helplessly.

"Clearly we are in similar situations."

"But I'm too confused about my own to understand, appreciate and advise you on yours!" the other said and they both nodded and giggled slightly.

"We have two choices."

"Yes. Take the flight. Or return."

"A part of me feels that going back could change everything. Another part warns that it could be the biggest mistake of my life"

"How do we decide...?"

"We could toss a coin!"

"But we toss and we call correctly. Do we both return? If it turns out to be a mistake wouldn't we both suffer?"

"On the other hand if we take the flight out of here we could be denying ourselves the life we've always wished for."

"So what do we do?"

The first shrugged. "Wait!" she gripped the other as an idea hit her. "Let's do this. We toss a coin but not as one, we toss against the other, as though we are adversaries. If you call heads and your call is true, you take the flight and I'll return. But if you call wrong you return and I take the flight. Okay?"

The other woman thought a bit. "But what if our decisions are not synced with our destiny? Suppose you fly out and I return while it should have been the other way around?"

They both thought about it. And that special intuitive sense told them they were doing the right thing. They felt deep in their hearts that that this action would lead them to the right solution. They smiled at each other as their eyes met and they felt a special sense of oneness. One of them pulled out a coin and tossed it. They looked at the result.

They got up, seeming much happier now. "It's decided now and I feel much lighter!"

"So do I. I feel things will now turn out right for both of us."

"Goodbye."

They realised they didn't know each other's names. Once again their eyes met and they smiled.

"I'm not going to give you my name or ask you for yours.... But remember me on your wedding day."

"I will. And if you find someone else, remember me on your wedding day as well!"

Each woman looked at the other, who had helped her make the most critical decision of her life.

"I'll never forget you, ever. Whenever I look up and see a lonely cloud floating high above, I'll remember you..."

------THE END------

About the Author

A career spent in studying and communicating to the Indian consumer has led the author to a better understanding of human motivations and why people do what they do. Emotions, he believes, is all that we are about. Emotions make us rise to situations and also fail them. And the better stories are ones which lays bare human flaws. It's these flaws that show us as vulnerable and make us relatable.

Rajan has lived out his life balancing his heart and his head. A night-school teacher, an entrepreneur at 23, and a decade-long stint as the CEO of an advertising agency, Rajan believes that his stories are the outcome of his varied interactions and experiences. When not writing, he's travelling the country by train. "There's a story in every journey."

Rajan lives in Mumbai with his wife and teenage son.